KING

Wallowing in bitterness and self-pity, Marnie had fled from her family and her fiancé to take refuge on a tiny Scottish island. She just wanted to be left alone; she resented any contact with anyone. But somehow she couldn't avoid the forceful Ewan McNeill. Wouldn't the man *ever* get the message?

KING OF
CULLA

BY

SALLY WENTWORTH

MILLS & BOON LIMITED
15–16 BROOK'S MEWS
LONDON W1A 1DR

First published 1981
Australian copyright 1981
Philippine copyright 1981
This edition 1981

© Sally Wentworth 1981

ISBN 0 263 73537 0

Set in Monophoto Plantin 10 on 12 pt.

*Made and printed in Great Britain by
Richard Clay (The Chaucer Press) Ltd,
Bungay, Suffolk*

CHAPTER ONE

'HERE, lassie, let me give you a hand.'

The crewman from the steamer went to pick up her suitcase, fearing that the girl wouldn't have the strength to carry it off the boat. It was a large case, and although the girl was tall, she looked so thin that he thought even a light breeze would knock her over, let alone the strong wind that was blowing now. But the girl merely said, 'I can manage, thank you,' in a polite, toneless voice, and picking up the case herself, carried it without too much effort out of the warmth of the heated cabin on to the open deck. Immediately the wind, which had travelled all the way across the Atlantic Ocean, gaining force as it went, caught at her, sending icy fingers of cold through her clothes, and making her shiver. It blew off the hood of her anorak and sent her long, honey-blonde hair flying into a golden aureole about her head as she turned her back to the wind and made her way to the gangplank.

It was more sheltered here in the harbour, but even so the steamer pitched alarmingly and she had to hold on tightly to the rail with her right hand as she walked down the steps to the jetty, giving a small sigh of relief as she found herself on dry land at last, although her legs still felt unnatural and wobbly after the long boat journey out from Oban.

After moving clear of the gangplank, the girl set down her case and paused to pull her hood up and tie the strings more tightly under her chin, pushing her

hair back under the protecting cover. She glanced up
at the sky, dark grey and heavy with low, fast-moving
rainclouds, a sky that would have daunted most travel-
lers and sent them hurrying on to their destinations,
but which didn't seem to affect this girl at all, in fact
she continued to gaze up at it for some time before
turning her attention to the port of Ardsay which lay
spread out before her at the end of the jetty.

Although she had formed no clear picture in her
mind, she had somehow supposed that any port on a
small island in the Outer Hebrides would be close-
clustered round the harbour, its houses built of grey
stone with slate roofs, the town merging into a sombre
background of grey hills that matched the cold sea and
the leaden sky. But, although there were several build-
ings at the foot of the jetty, the rest of the town—not
much bigger than an English village—sprawled along
two or three side roads, and the houses, instead of
being of a uniform greyness, were architecturally different and often had walls painted white or other light
colours under roofs of warm red tiles. Admittedly the
hills that rose above the town were dark grey with
drifts of winter snow still on the highest areas, with no
warmth yet in the March winds to melt them, and the
sea and the sky were all that she expected, but looking
at the town the girl felt somehow cheated. It *ought* to
be cold and forbidding, the houses had no right to look
bright and homely. For a moment she had misgivings;
maybe she had been wrong to come here to the little
island of Culla.

Slowly the girl bent to pick up her case again and
walk down the jetty. The man on the steamer had been
wrong, it really wasn't very heavy. She smiled rather
grimly to herself; it was surprising how little space a

lifetime could take up.

There was a solitary and rather elderly taxi waiting at the end of the jetty under the partial cover of an overhang of a large, warehouse-type building, but it was empty, the driver nowhere to be seen. The girl waited by it for several minutes in growing impatience and increasing cold. There were several people about, warmly wrapped against the wind, and they looked at her curiously as they passed, until she began to feel embarrassed just standing there like a lemon. For all she knew the driver might have stopped work for the day and she could stand here for hours waiting. Almost angrily she tried the door and found it to be open, then pressed the horn loudly several times. For a while nothing happened, then the door of a small café on the other side of the road opened and a man came out, shrugging himself into a thick overcoat.

The man ambled over and looked her up and down with open interest. 'Is it you be wantin' a taxi now?'

'Yes,' the girl agreed shortly, refraining from adding that it should have been perfectly obvious.

'And where did you be wantin' to go?' he asked as he picked up her case and carefully put it in the boot, unhurriedly arranging it to his satisfaction.

The girl got in the back and waited for him to get in before saying, 'First I'd like to go to the Culla Estate office, please.'

The driver turned to look at her, his face alight with inquisitiveness. 'Is it the factor now you'll be seeing? And maybe you'll be the one that's taken the house over at Taornish, then? Morag Ferguson was telling as how she was getting the house ready.'

Frowning, the girl cut him short. 'Just drive me to the office, please.'

Reluctantly the man obeyed, but talking all the time. 'Yon's a nice house, although it's about four miles from Ardsay and the bus doesna' go there. But it has the electricity, and Willy Mackenzie who keeps the grocery shop has sent a load of food to fill the freezer. Enough for several people, he said. Be you going to stay there with your family, lassie?'

A strange look, almost of pain, flicked across the girl's face, but was quickly hidden. 'Are we nearly there yet?' she demanded snappily, ignoring his question.

'Aye, it's just round the next corner.'

They continued on a little farther and he pulled up outside what looked like an ordinary house, but which had a wooden sign with 'CULLA ESTATE OFFICE, FACTOR: IAN MACDONALD' painted on it and fixed on one side of the door.

'I'll be coming in with you to wait in the warm,' the taxi driver told her, and began to open his door.

'No. You can wait here,' the girl ordered abruptly, guessing that the man merely wished to satisfy his curiosity about her. She got out of the old car, crossed to the door, which gave directly on to the pavement, and pressed an old-fashioned brass bellpush. After a few minutes a light came on in the window arch over the doorway and then the door was opened by a thin woman in her early fifties.

'I'd like to see the factor, please.'

The woman smiled. 'Come you in then, lassie. I'm Mrs MacDonald.' She saw the taxi waiting outside and gave a nod and a wave to the driver before shutting the door again. 'The office is down here.'

She led the way down the hall and opened a door on

the left. 'Ian, someone to see you.'

The house was warm and the girl pushed the hood back off her head. Mrs MacDonald glanced at her as she stood aside to let her enter the office, and then her eyes widened as she took in the beauty of the girl's face with its perfect bone structure of wide forehead, straight nose and high cheekbones, and pale lips with just a hint of sensuality in the lower one. But it was her eyes that held Mrs MacDonald's gaze the most; eyes of a deep, deep blue, fringed by long, dark lashes that reminded the island woman of a rock pool lost in the deep shade of the cliff but with traces of the golden sun still in its depths. The woman hastily withdrew her gaze, aware that she was staring, and it was only later, as she walked back to her kitchen, that she realised how white the girl had looked, her eyes dark-shadowed and looking over-large in a face so thin that it could almost be described as gaunt.

Her husband, too, was forming the same opinion as he rose and reached out to shake the girl's hand.

She returned his handshake almost reluctantly and said curtly, 'My name is Adams, Marnie Adams. I arranged to lease a house at Taornish from you through my solicitors.' She fished inside the bag slung over her shoulder and handed the factor a sheet of paper. 'This is a copy of the letter you sent acknowledging receipt of the cheque for the lease.'

Mr MacDonald took the letter, glanced at it briefly, and handed it back. 'Aye, that's quite in order, Miss Adams. I'll get you the keys.' He moved rather ponderously to a small safe in the corner and selected a bunch of three keys tied with a label saying 'TAORNISH COTTAGE' on it. 'Here you are then, lassie.'

'Thank you.' Marnie picked up the keys and slipped them in her bag. 'I take it that all the supplies I asked for have been delivered to the house?'

'Och aye, enough for a small army,' the man smiled. 'Food, and peats and fuel for the electricity generator. And Morag Ferguson, who lives in a croft nearby, has been in and cleaned and made the place ready for you.' He raised his eyebrows. 'But you'll not be living up at Taornish alone, surely?'

She met his look squarely, 'Yes, I shall be quite alone.'

He opened his mouth as if to say something more, but the cold, aloof look on the girl's face made the words die in his throat. As he looked at her he thought that hers was the most beautiful face he'd ever seen— and the saddest. She looked as if fate had dealt her more blows than she could take and that she was haunted by grief and unhappiness.

The factor was not a fanciful man and he tried to shake off the mood. Perhaps she had just been ill and had come to the Hebrides to rest and recuperate; many people did so. Trying to be kind, he said, 'I'm sure my wife has the kettle boiling by now; will you stay and take a cup or two of tea with us before you go to the cottage? We could tell you something of Culla and your neighbours at Taornish.'

Marnie frowned. 'I thought the place was supposed to be isolated?'

'Oh, it is. There's no' but five or six houses there and all separated by the land around each croft. You'll no' be disturbed, if that's what you want.'

'That's what I want,' the girl affirmed. She moved towards the door.

'Will you no' stay for some tea?'

'No, thank you, I prefer to get to the cottage. Goodbye.'

'Goodbye, Miss Adams. And *fàilte do'duthaich*.' Then, seeing her frown, he said, 'It's Gaelic; it means welcome to the country.'

'Oh.' She nodded awkwardly. 'Thank you.'

He followed her to the front door, but shut it quickly behind her as the wind gusted in. Marnie paused for a moment on the step. Although it was only about four-thirty in the afternoon, the leaden sky had made the day almost dark and already squares of light shone out from the windows of houses and the few shops nearby. There was hardly anyone out on the streets now, just a few people hurrying along, bent against the wind, eager to get inside out of the cold.

Quickly Marnie got into the car again. 'Taornish Cottage now, please.'

The driver gave a kind of snort that distinctly said, 'I told you so,' and started to drive out of the town.

For a while they drove parallel to the sea and Marnie tried to look out at the scenery, but it was too dark and she was too tired from the journey to care much anyway. There was plenty of time, she could look tomorrow—there would be a million tomorrows. Another, all too familiar, wave of despair engulfed her, a sadness so fierce that it was like a knife pressing into an open wound. She closed her eyes, leaning back in the seat and balling her hands into tight fists as she tried to think of something else, anything but that. She would think of the cottage. Yes. Would it be ready for her as she'd instructed, would it be as she'd imagined from the estate agent's description and the one small and rather blurred photograph that she'd seen? She forced her mind to go through the description again: a

fifty-year-old converted croft with one large room and
a kitchen downstairs and two bedrooms and bathroom
set under a gabled roof upstairs. Surrounded by
approximately an acre of land and with various outhouses, which sounded delightfully vague. There had
been far more detail about the house itself, of course,
but what had made Marnie decide on the spur of the
moment to take the house had been the part where it
said, 'Situated on the west coast of the island, in an
isolated but sheltered bay surrounded by hills and
some distance from public transportation and nearest
village.'

It was that that her soul craved; to be completely
alone and away from well-meaning friends who gave
unwanted comfort and said that time would help. But
it wasn't true, it just got worse as time went on ...
She caught herself up abruptly. No, don't think of that,
think of the cottage. Go through the list of stores that
she'd ordered. Now, what was it: soups, ham, vegetables ...

Marnie was concentrating so hard, her eyes still tight
shut, that she was hardly aware that the taxi had slowed
and the driver was speaking to her. She opened her
eyes, blinking in the darkness and trying to peer out.
'Are we there already?'

'No, but here is Ewan McNeill who also has a house in
Taornish and I'm thinking we'll be giving him a lift.'

Before Marnie could protest, he had stopped the car
and wound down his window, calling out something in
Gaelic to a man who was striding along, a heavy-look-
ing sack thrown over his shoulder and a large dog at
his heels.

The man came to the side of the car and exchanged
a greeting, bending down low to see in. In the small

illumination given by the dashboard lights it was difficult to see him clearly, but Marnie got the impression
that he was tall and broad, his dark hair blown into
disarray by the wind.

''Tis your lucky day now, Ewan. Here I am taking
the new tenant to Taornish Cottage and we can be
taking you up right to your door.'

'Now just a minute,' Marnie interrupted forcefully.
'You're under hire to me, and I don't choose to share
the taxi, so will you please drive on?'

Both men turned to look at her in some surprise.
Almost as if she was a piece of luggage that had dared
to speak, Marnie thought resentfully. But it was *her*
taxi, and the last thing she wanted was to share it with
someone who would want to talk and ask her questions.

The driver opened his mouth and started to say, 'But
you dinna' understand, lassie . . .' but the other man
lifted a hand to silence him.

'It's no matter, Hector,' he said, his accent English,
not Hebridean, 'I'm enjoying the walk. And the lady is
probably tired and eager to get home. But I'll let you
carry my load for me.' He passed the sack through the
window and looked at her. 'You won't object to letting
Hector do that, I trust?'

Marnie found herself looking into a pair of dark,
rather sardonic eyes, the left eyebrow raised quiz-
zically, as if the man knew darn well that she was just
being awkward and daring her to defy him.

Tightly she answered, 'No, I don't object to that.'

He nodded, said something else she didn't understand to the driver and then they were on their way
again, the man and his dog left behind them in the
gathering darkness of night and storm.

After another mile it began to rain, large, heavy drops that spattered loudly against the windows and made the driver slow down as he peered through the windscreen, the wipers squeaking protestingly every time they cleared an arc of glass only to have it immediately obscured again. The driver muttered something under his breath, about 'wouldn'a hurt to give Ewan a lift,' but Marnie refused to feel guilty; the man had looked big and tough, a shower of rain wouldn't hurt him. The road had been running inland, but now they turned off the main, tarmacked road on to a narrower side road that ran under the steep side of a high, craggy hill, almost lost now in the darkness, and then sloped gently down towards the sea again. Marnie saw the lights of one or two houses on her left, standing well back from the road and with some distance between them, then the taxi slowed down and came to a stop. Marnie peered out of the window but couldn't see a thing.

'Is this it?' she asked dubiously.

'Aye. That'll be two pounds.'

She gave him the money together with a tip, but he made no move to open the door for her or to get her case so she had to heave it out of the boot herself. A punishment because she wouldn't share the taxi with his friend, she supposed. Immediately she'd got the case out he drove away, and Marnie had to step nimbly out of the way to avoid being splashed with mud thrown up by his tyres. He turned the car and drove past her again, and for a moment, in the blaze of his headlights, Marnie had her first glimpse of Taornish Cottage, her new home, a grey stone building with the door set squarely in the centre and a window on either side. The slate roof came down low, and set into it were three small gable windows immediately over the door and windows on the lower floor. Then the car was gone and Marnie was left alone in the dark.

As the sound of the car engine receded, she became aware of a curious pounding noise, ahead of her and over to the left somewhere, and for a few minutes she listened to it intently, oblivious of the driving rain, wondering what on earth it could be. Then it came to her: of course, it was the sea! Somewhere, not very far away, it must strike against a cliff or headland, creating this even booming noise as each wave crashed against the rock and then drew back only to thunder forward yet again. Impossible to see the sea, impossible to see anything in this close darkness now that the car had gone. Marnie supposed she should have asked the driver to wait and light her way to the front door for her, although he was quite likely to have refused, the mood he was in.

Grimly she picked up her case and edged forward, feeling for the gap in the low stone wall that surrounded the house, and then groped her way up the path to the front door in the pouring rain. Cursing her lack of foresight in not bringing a torch, she felt around the door for the keyhole and then found it on the other side of the door, in completely the opposite place to where she'd expected to find it. With a sigh of relief she pushed open the door, dragged her case inside, and then pushed the door to behind her, grateful that the long journey from London was over and to be out of the rain and wind at last.

For a moment she just sagged back against the door, feeling cold and wet, and tired right through to her bones, then she became aware that the room was warm and of the glow of a fire that was banked low in the stone fireplace. It gave off a gentle, flickering light that revealed a comfy-looking settee covered in a flowered material over by the far wall, and a table with four chairs grouped round it set under the heavily curtained window to her left. Marnie moved towards the warmth as if drawn by a magnet, kneeling down on the hearth-rug and pulling off her wet gloves to hold her hands out to the fire. There weren't many flames, just the steady heat from what looked like thick squares of wood. She picked up the long metal rod and poked at the fire gingerly. No, it wasn't wood, and it certainly wasn't coal, which would have given off a far greater heat. Then one of the blocks fell apart and she could see the black fibrous mass more clearly: of course, this must be peat. She'd read about it often; in books Highlanders were always out cutting peat blocks to dry for the winter, but she'd never seen any before.

With the fire burning more brightly, Marnie turned to take stock of her surroundings. She found a light switch over by the door and in the better light saw that the room also contained another armchair covered in the same flowered chintz, a long wooden sideboard with a mirror over it, and in the alcove on the right-hand side of the fireplace a row of shelves mostly filled with books. The left-hand alcove, in pride of place, contained a small table with a television set on it. This last surprised her a little; she thought she'd got far enough away from civilisation to be free of piped entertainment, but obviously not; where there was electricity television was sure to follow. Then she shrugged. What did it matter, she didn't have to watch it, and she could always lose the thing in a cupboard or one of the various outhouses somewhere.

A draught blowing through the crack between the

door and the jamb made her shiver and she hastened
to pull the curtain across, the brass rings jingling on
the metal rod. Slowly Marnie unzipped her anorak and
hung it on a hook on the wall. She supposed she ought
to have something to eat, she hadn't eaten since breakfast that morning, but she didn't feel hungry; she
hadn't felt hungry since the accident three months ago.
Such a short time really, and yet it felt as if she'd lived
a dozen lifetimes since then, first in the hospital and
then trying to rebuild her life again, until she'd
realised, suddenly, that she just couldn't go on, that
she had to get right away from everyone and everything
she'd ever known. That, or swallow all the sleeping
pills the doctor had given her in one go and put an end
to this living hell!

Hurriedly Marnie ran towards the door in the far
wall, turned on the light on the other side of the door
and found herself in the kitchen. She began to open
cupboards, almost feverishly forcing herself to concentrate on their contents and to choose something to eat.
She found a tin of soup and an old-fashioned opener
in one of the kitchen drawers, the sort where you had
to bang the point in. She hadn't used one before, she'd
had an electric opener at the flat; not that she'd ever
used it much, there had always been some man eager
to take her out for a meal when Alan wasn't around,
happy to escort such a stunning-looking girl who drew
all eyes wherever she went.

The tin lid, by the time she'd managed to open it
enough to get the contents out, was hopelessly
mangled, and Marnie looked at it in some disgust. God,
she couldn't even open a tin! Tears pricked her eyes
and she had to blink hard to keep them back. She was
just exhausted from the journey, that was all. She'd be

fine when she'd eaten and had a good sleep. Luckily
the cooker was electric and presented no problem.
While the soup was heating she forced herself to have
a slower look at the stock of food. Yes, there was
everything here she'd ordered, plus a few things more
besides. She'd certainly never asked for flour or yeast
or baking power. Did someone expect her to make
bread and cakes? She'd never made either in her life,
and certainly didn't intend to start now when they
could be stored ready-made in the large freezer that
took up most of the space in the kitchen.

The soup was bubbling and Marnie turned off the
hotplate, then noticed that the oven was turned on low.
Picking up a teatowel, she opened the door and was·
immediately met by the most mouthwatering smell of
cooking. Inside, a casserole, chicken by the look of it,
simmered gently in a glass ovenware dish, and above it
on a higher shelf, there was a pie, its pastry sugared
and golden, smelling of apples and cloves.

Uncertainly Marnie stood up, a frown on her face.
She opened a cupboard to look for a soup bowl and
saw a note propped up against a bread bin. It was
written in English and said, 'Welcome to Taornish.
I'll call round in the morning to see if you need anything else' and was signed Morag Ferguson.

Anger surged through Marnie like a hot wave. How
dared this woman presume to cook for her? All she'd
asked for was for the provisions she'd ordered to be
delivered to the house. She hadn't asked for the fire to
be lit or a meal prepared. And now this Morag
Ferguson person had said that she'd be calling tomorrow. To sit and drink tea and ask her questions until
she'd wormed everything out of her, Marnie supposed
furiously. And what good would it be then to have got

away from everyone who knew her and knew about the accident? She might just as well have stayed in London and locked herself in her flat. Only she'd tried that and it hadn't worked; there had been too many memories of Alan—and of Sue.

Marnie slumped down in a chair by the kitchen table, staring at the food in the cooker, then suddenly furious again, kicked the door shut viciously and turned off the heat. She'd be darned if she'd have this woman interfering in her life when she'd come so far to get away, prying into her business and clucking round her like an old hen! Providing groceries she hadn't ordered and cooking food she didn't want. Angrily Marnie went round the cupboards and pulled out all the things she hadn't ordered and piled them on the kitchen table. Flour, yeast, baking powder, porridge—yeuk, she never touched the stuff—oatmeal, jam, milk and cheese out of the fridge, a loaf of still warm home-made bread from the bread bin. Finding an empty cardboard box, Marnie piled it all inside. When the casserole and pie were cold, they too could go in, and tomorrow she would hand the lot back, and then perhaps this Ferguson woman would get the message and leave her alone.

She took her soup back into the sitting-room and, turning off the light, sat on the hearthrug by the fire, her back leaning against the settee. Slowly she drank the soup, gazing, almost mesmerised, into the blue and gold flames given off by the peat. But then pictures began to form in the flames and she hastily turned her head away and drank the rest of the soup down, feeling no better for the hot liquid. She looked round to see if there was some sort of guard to put in front of the fire, but couldn't see one. Then she thought, oh, hell, what does it matter if the place burns down, anyway?

Picking up her suitcase, Marnie opened the other door which gave off the sitting-room and climbed the narrow windowless staircase leading to the upper floor. Pushing open the first door she came to, she saw that this was a smallish bedroom with two single beds in it, with a narrow gap between them, and hardly any space left for the heavy wardrobe and dressing-table. The room on the other side of the landing, over the top of the sitting-room, was much bigger and contained a large double bed with a beautifully made patchwork quilt thrown over it. Here, too, there was a wardrobe and rather old-fashioned dressing-table, the type with three mirrors so that you could see yourself from all sides. There were fires alight in both bedrooms, so obviously the woman who'd got the house ready had been expecting several people.

Marnie dumped her case down in the middle of the larger room. She supposed she ought to unpack, but there would be plenty of time in the morning; she could take all day if she felt like it. There would be no well-meaning friends calling round to try and console her or wanting to take her out to try and take her mind off her unhappiness. No one to disturb the solitude. Except, she remembered, this prying woman who would be coming tomorrow. Well, she would just have to get rid of her and make it plain that she wasn't wanted, and then, perhaps, she would be left in peace.

She sorted out a nightdress from among the jeans and sweaters in her case and began to undress. The bathroom, set between the two bedrooms, had only an electric fire fixed high on the wall, to heat it, and as this hadn't been turned on, it was icy cold, and Marnie soon ran back shivering, her bare feet frozen, to the warmth of the bedroom. Automatically she took off her wristwatch and placed it on the bedside cabinet where she would be able to see it easily in the morning. Then she paused, staring down at it. It was a very good watch, solid gold, a present for her last birthday, her twenty-third. From Alan. A gift which she'd accepted happily, not knowing that even then he was no longer in love with her. Abruptly Marnie picked up the watch and dropped it into the top drawer of the cabinet. What did time matter any more? To her it no longer had any meaning, especially here on Culla. She would eat when she felt hungry and sleep when she was tired, and lie in bed all day if she didn't feel like getting up. What was there to get up for anyway—now?

Hesitantly she glanced towards her bandbag. Should she take some of the sleeping pills the doctor at the hospital had prescribed for her? She'd had to up to now because it was the only way she had been able to get any sleep, but tonight she felt so utterly weary, tired enough to sleep for a week. Surely tonight she wouldn't need them?

Pushing aside the covers, Marnie climbed into the bed and found a hot water bottle there taking the chill off sheets that smelt of lavender, and faintly of something else. She pressed her nose into the pillow, trying to trace the subtle fragrance. Then it came to her. Yes, that was it; they smelt tangy like the sea, as if they had been hung to dry in the warm clear breeze that had drifted over the ocean to this tiny island and which now blew around the house, rattling the window panes and sending waves thudding against the nearby shore. Marnie listened to them for only a short while, the hot water bottle cuddled to her chest, then drifted off into an exhausted but restless sleep.

The car was sliding, sliding down a long, winding spiral of road that went on and on for miles and miles. Beside her Sue was shouting at her and pulling at her hands, dislodging them from the steering wheel as Marnie fought to keep hold of it. And then there were other cars, coming at her from every direction, and the noise, the terrible noise, echoing all around her until she couldn't stand it any more and had to take her hands off the steering wheel and put them over her ears. The quiet then was wonderful, wonderful, until she heard Sue screaming. She turned to Sue to tell her to stop, but when she looked she saw that it wasn't Sue at all, it couldn't be Sue, because where her face had been there was just a mask of blood, blood that streamed everywhere, everywhere . . .

Marnie's scream of horror echoed round the bedroom and she sat up with a start, white and trembling, beads of perspiration standing out on her forehead, her clothes clinging to her. For a moment she couldn't think where she was and stared into the darkness, eyes wide and terrified. But when she caught sight of the glowing embers of the dying fire and realisation came flooding back. Oh God, no, not the nightmare again! Waking, sleeping, must she live with it for the rest of her life? Or until she couldn't stand it any more and put an end to them for ever?

Still shaking, she leant back against the wooden headboard, knowing that natural sleep was impossible now. It was her own fault, she should have taken the sleeping pills. If she took enough of them they knocked her out so completely that she didn't dream at all. She groped for her watch and then remembered she'd put it in the drawer. Only just after midnight. Getting out

of bed, Marnie picked up her bag and took out the
bottle of pills. How many should she take? She'd been
prescribed two, but with two the nightmares could get
through. She swallowed four and got back into bed,
willing herself not to think until her eyes began to close
and she fell into a deep sleep, the nightmares sup-
pressed beneath the strong drugs.

A loud knocking sound penetrated through the heavy
fog of sleep and Marnie pushed herself up in bed, still
half-bemused, her mind fuddled by a sleep that had
done her little good. The knocking came again and she
struggled out of bed. Then she heard the front door
open and a female voice call, 'Is there anyone in the
house?'

Hastily now, Marnie pulled a housecoat out of her
open suitcase, scattering its contents on the floor as
she did so, then ran out of the bedroom and down the
stairs to the sitting-room. A rather buxom woman in
early middle age, her dark hair beginning to show grey
at the front, was pulling open the curtains to let the
daylight flood in. She turned as Marnie came into the
room and gave her a warm smile. '*Ceud mile fàilte,*' the
woman said to her, then laughed. 'Och, I'm sorry, that
means a hundred thousand welcomes. Did I wake you
now, lassie?' She moved towards the fire. 'But it's after
ten o'clock, and when I saw that there was no smoke
coming from your chimneys I thought I'd come and
show you how to make up your fires. Did you not
bank them up last night?'

She bent to pick up the poker, but stopped when
Marnie said abruptly, 'Who are you? How did you get
in?'

The woman straightened, a look of surprise on her
face. 'Why, I'm Morag Ferguson. Did you not find

my note? And I have a key that the factor gave me.'

Marnie held out her hand, her face set. 'Give it to me, please.'

Mrs Ferguson looked at her in bewilderment. 'But I always have a key so that I can make sure the house is clean and ready for the tenants.'

'But as I've taken the cottage that won't be necessary, will it?' Marnie pointed out coldly. 'The key, please.'

Slowly the woman groped in the pocket of her thick tweed coat, her face troubled. She looked at Marnie with some misgivings as she reluctantly handed her the key. 'You'll no be meaning to lock your door?'

'I most certainly do,' Marnie retorted shortly.

'But why, lassie? This is no' London. There's no one here will want to steal from you or—or harm you in any way. You've no cause to be afeared. No one locks their doors on Culla.'

Marnie pulled her thin housecoat closer around her, the cold making her shiver. 'I'm not afraid,' she answered snappily. 'I just want to be sure of privacy.'

The elder woman looked distressed. 'But lassie, the factor phoned me up last night and said you were going to live here alone and not with your family as we'd all expected. If you're going to be by yourself then you'll be needing help to show you how to go on in a croft, how to bank up your fires so that they never go out, and how to work the generator and plant your seeds for the summer and . . .'

'I don't need any help,' Marnie broke in forcefully. 'I can manage perfectly well by myself.'

Mrs Ferguson started to protest, but Marnie turned and hurried into the kitchen where she took the now cold casserole and pie from the oven and put them in

the box with the other unwanted groceries. She carried
it into the sitting-room and thrust it at the older woman
so that she had to take it.

'Why, what's this?'

'These are the groceries that you laid in on your
own initiative. I certainly didn't order them and I
won't be using them.'

The island woman looked into the box and then
stared at her round-eyed. 'Not be making bread or
cakes? But how then will you . . .'

'And I also didn't ask for a meal to be prepared,'
Marnie went on, ignoring her interruption, adding
coldly, 'If I had wanted the services of a cook I would
have asked for one when I leased the cottage.'

Colour flooded into Morag Ferguson's cheeks and
her back stiffened, then she looked at Marnie's too-
thin features and dark-shadowed eyes and her face
softened again. 'Look, lassie,' she began, 'I dinna ken
what it is that's the matter, but . . .'

'There's nothing the matter with me,' Marnie broke
in rudely. She crossed to the front door and opened it.
'Thank you for getting the house ready yesterday, Mrs
Ferguson, but I shan't need your help ever again.
Goodbye.'

Even after such downright bluntness the elder
woman still hesitated, but Marnie stood waiting impatiently, her face set, and Mrs Ferguson gave a help-
less sort of shrug and carried the box out of the house.

Immediately she had crossed the threshold Marnie
slammed the door shut behind her and turned the key
in the lock, her fingers trembling with reaction. Then
she rushed to the window to hide behind the net curtains while she watched to see what the woman would
do.

Mrs Ferguson walked slowly down the path and awkwardly opened the gate with the box in her hands. In the roadway she turned left, to go inland, but had only gone a few steps when she seemed to change her mind and turned round decisively. Marnie thought that she was coming back and shrank away from the window, but the island woman walked quickly by without once looking towards the cottage and hurried up the road to another house a hundred yards or so farther on on the left-hand side of the road. Marnie hadn't realised it was there last night in the darkness, but now she saw that it looked quite a substantial place, built of grey stone and two-storeyed like her own, but it looked fairly new and much larger from what she could see of it. The woman went up to the house, knocked on the door, then pushed it open and walked in. Gone to have a good gossip about me, I suppose, Marnie thought resentfully, then shrugged: let them talk all they wanted as long as they left her alone. She watched for a few minutes but was freezing in just her nightdress and housecoat, so she ran upstairs to dress in jeans and a thick sweater, all the while keeping an eye on the other house through the window. Downstairs again, she made herself a mug of coffee and had time to nearly finish it before she saw Mrs Ferguson leave the other house, minus the box this time, and walk back down the road until she disappeared round a bend.

Marnie gave her ten minutes in case she changed her mind and came back, then put on a pair of wellington boots and her anorak and wound a woolly scarf round her head. If she didn't get out of this house for a while, she'd stifle.

The wind plucked at the ends of her scarf, but it

was nowhere near as fierce as it had been the previous
day. The rain had gone and the sky, although still
cloudy, was quite light. She turned to the right, towards the pounding waves and the sea, and hurried
along the uneven road. The vivid green of grass was
starting to show through the black, peaty soil in the
fields leading up to the hills and seagulls rose into the
air as she passed, wheeling and screaming through the
sky.

As she passed the other house a dog began to bark
and then a big, chestnut-coloured Great Dane came
lolloping towards her. Marnie stood still and turned to
face it. The animal was as big as a small pony and
easily came up as high as her waist. A shout from
the house made the dog come to a sudden halt and it
stood, its teeth bared, growling softly. A man came out
of the garden of the house and began to walk towards
them. Marnie recognised the man they'd overtaken in
the taxi the previous night; what was it the driver had
called him—McNeill?

'Don't be afraid,' he called out. 'The dog won't hurt
you.'

Marnie turned and began to run along the road towards the sea. It wasn't animals she was afraid of, she
could cope with them. It was just people that she
couldn't stand.

CHAPTER TWO

THE road ran on between fields for another hundred yards or so, but these gradually became increasingly rock-strewn until the road was bounded by large out-crops of grey rock on either side which came up close on to its edge, so that it was almost like walking through a roofless tunnel. Marnie rounded a bend in the road and suddenly the rocks ended and she was in the open again with the sea lying spread out before her only fifty yards or so away. The shore formed a shallow bay, shelving gently over a white sandy beach in front of her but with steep cliffs running down from the hills on the right-hand arm. The tide was out, but still the waves beat against the cliffs, only more gently than last night, now that the storm had blown itself out.

Slowly Marnie followed the road until it petered out near what must once have been a stone jetty but which now lay broken and crumbled by the strength of thousands of winter tides. It surprised her that there was sand in the bay; she had expected it to be covered with rocks and pebbles, to be a harsh and forbidding place, but this sand was as white and soft as any on a Mediterranean beach. Why, you could even imagine families coming here to paddle and picnic in the summer, their laughter echoing round the cliffs as the cries of the sea birds echoed now. She kicked irritably at a pebble. This wasn't what she had expected when she'd decided to come here; she had wanted cold and hard solitude, not pleasant beaches and people who wished her a thousand welcomes at every turn.

Turning to the right, Marnie walked nearer to the cliffs, where the sea swirled angrily at their foot, caught in a maelstrom of currents. Debris littered the shore here, spewed up by the last tide: pieces of wood and a few lumps of coal, rusting tins thrown overboard by some passing ship. The breeze was stronger here, plucking at her scarf and blowing stray strands of hair into her eyes, but it suited her mood and she walked nearer to the cliffs. Above her she saw a small cavelike cleft between two rocks and climbed up to huddle inside, sheltered from the wind.

For a while she gazed out at the sea, fascinated by its continuous motion, its everlasting strength as it sent wave after wave dashing against the rocks, surging up their sheer sides in clouds of spray and then sucking the water back only to send in yet another wave. This was probably only a normal spring tide, but to Marnie the sea looked dark and angry. It was certainly a hell of a lot different from the placid Thames which had flowed nearby her Chelsea flat and which she had always taken for granted, only really seeing it when she had been invited to a floating party on one of the many luxurious motor-cruisers moored along its banks. She remembered one party that she'd been to with Alan, although he hadn't really wanted to come; he'd been taking his exams then and had wanted to study, but she'd insisted he escorted her. Then, when the party was at its height, someone had quietly started up the engines and taken the boat down the estuary and wouldn't turn back until the next day. Alan had been furious, she remembered, one of the few times she'd seen him angry, but nowhere near as furious as that last time, when he'd accused her of deliberately killing the woman he loved.

Marnie shut her eyes tightly and put her balled fists against her temples, shutting out the pictures. But that was the wrong thing to do. What was it the psychiatrist at the hospital had said: 'You'll never be able to forget what happened, so you're going to have to learn to live with it, to accept it. Don't keep trying to shut it out.' Shut it out—as if she could, Marnie thought dejectedly. But perhaps he was right, maybe if she let it go through her mind again it would help to lay the ghost, the ghost that stood at the foot of her bed every night, the ghost whose face was a mask of blood.

Fiercely she closed her eyes and forced her mind to go reluctantly back, back to last year when the world had been a sane and wonderful place, a time when she had been loved and secure and when nothing could possibly go wrong. She had been so happy that day driving down to spend Christmas at home with her father and the stepmother who had taken the place of the mother she'd never known. Marnie remembered she was excited because she'd just won a contract to model clothes for a French fashion house and she was to go to Paris for three months as well as receiving a substantial fee. On the strength of it she'd been extravagant with Christmas presents: a piece of porcelain to add to her collection for her stepmother, some bottles of vintage wine for Daddy, and Christian Dior perfume for Sue, her elder sister by two years who worked in the local library and who was so staid and never went out on dates. And for Alan she had gold cufflinks with his initials engraved on them. Darling Alan, it would be lovely to see him, although she did hope he wouldn't ask her again to set a wedding date; she really would like to do this contract with the French house first and who knew what that might lead

to? And there was plenty of time, they had all the time
in the world.

She loved Alan very much, of course, had done so
almost from the time he had moved into the neighbourhood and Sue had brought him home. Her sister
had been nineteen then and Alan her very first boy-
friend. But he had taken one look at Marnie, just blos-
soming into young womanhood and beautiful even
then, and a bright, glowing contrast to her plainer
sister, and had fallen head over heels in love with her.
They had been too young to marry then, of course;
Marnie was still at school and Alan training to become
a vet, but he had insisted that they become engaged
and had sold his secondhand car in order to buy her
the diamond solitaire which she wore on her left hand.
That had been over five years ago and Alan had passed
his exams long since, but by then Marnie had got
caught up in her own career as a model, and they
needed to save up to buy a house and it seemed silly to
give up her career when they could use the money. So
they had drifted on, Marnie quite content for the
moment to enjoy doing work she loved and the relative
fame that went with it. To be courted and flattered by
men but to have Alan safely in the background, a sheet
anchor who was always there whenever she needed
him, safe and dependable, undemanding except some,
rather exciting, times when they were alone together
and he lost control a little and begged her to marry
him. 'Now. Now, Marnie. Can't you see how much I
need you?'

Marnie stirred in her perch, looking bleakly out to
sea, Alan's words echoing in her brain like the seagulls'
cries. But she hadn't seen, hadn't seen at all until it
was too late, had merely laughed and kissed him, pro-

mising him everything he wanted, but not yet, wait just a little while longer, there was plenty of time.

She supposed she should have realised as soon as she got home that Christmas Eve. There was a strained atmosphere in the air and Sue could hardly look at her. And her father, whose favourite Marnie had always been, was especially kind and loving towards her. In the evening Alan, who had a practice in the town, arrived for dinner, and Marnie had run to greet him, lifting her face up happily for his kiss and hugging him exuberantly. So happy, so very happy. She hadn't even thought anything of it when he had only lightly returned her kiss, a worried frown on his face and a guarded look in his eyes.

The meal had been a difficult one with only Marnie talking naturally, telling them animatedly of an assignment in South America from which she'd just returned, only her father doing his best to join in, the others sitting quietly, hardly eating, smiling perfunctorily when she addressed them, but the smiles not reaching their eyes.

It was after dinner, when they had all moved into the sitting-room, that the blow was dealt. Her father had poured out drinks for them all while they sat round the fire, then, after a long, heavy, silence, her step-mother had suddenly burst out, 'It's wrong. We can't go on like this until after Christmas, pretending that nothing's happened.' She turned to her husband who had made a gesture to silence her. 'I know you wanted Marnie to have a happy holiday, but you must see that it isn't fair on Sue and Alan. She *has* to be told.'

'Told? What am I to be told?' Marnie asked, looking from one to the other of them. 'Oh, dear, you all look so serious.' She said it half-laughingly, thinking that it was some small thing they were worried about; that they'd arranged to go somewhere she might not want to, or something equally trivial.

Alan stood up as her stepmother spoke and put down his drink. He moved across to her chair and said rather unsteadily, 'I think I'd better talk to Marnie alone.'

Immediately Sue was on her feet. 'No! I'm staying too.'

Marnie stared up at them, only now beginning to realise that something was very wrong. 'What is it? What's happened?'

Her father took hold of his wife's arm. 'We'll go in the other room. Marnie, my dear child . . .' He looked at her rather helplessly and then walked quickly out of the room, her stepmother following more reluctantly.

Marnie got slowly to her feet and stood looking at her sister and her fiancé. Both of them looked very pale and she saw now that there were dark smudges round Sue's eyes. Even before Alan spoke she guessed what he was going to say.

'Marnie, I'm sorry, but I have to ask you to release me from our engagement. I want to marry Sue.' She could only stare at him speechlessly and after a moment he went on, 'It's something that's been growing between us gradually, but two months ago it came to a head and we realised that we were in love and . . .'

Anger suddenly shot through her and she interrupted him, her voice heavy with contempt, 'Don't bother to go on. Do you think I want to hear all the details of how my sister seduced my fiancé behind my back? Do you think I want to know that you were weak enough to listen to her?' she shouted at him. 'What did she do—flatter you, make sure she was always around? My God, I trusted you. I trusted *both* of you!'

She turned angrily away, unable to look at them, and Alan came up behind her. 'Marnie, please, try to understand. There were times when I needed you, needed you desperately, but you were always in London or abroad somewhere. It got so damned lonely sometimes that I . . .'

'Lonely?' Marnie burst out, swinging round to face him. 'And don't you think that I ever got lonely? That I needed you?'

He stared at her, a dark look in his eyes, then slowly shook his head. 'No, I don't. I think you were too wrapped up in your career to miss me at all. If you had, I think we'd have married years ago.'

Marnie glared at him. 'All right, you've made your point. Did you have to go to this length to get what you wanted? To drag Sue into it?'

He frowned. 'What do you mean?'

'I mean that okay, we'll get married.' Her voice softened. 'Just as soon as it can be arranged, if that's what you want?'

'Marnie!' Alan stared down at her wonderingly as she gave a little smile and put her hands on his chest.

'No!' Suddenly Sue caught hold of her arm and pulled her away. 'He doesn't want you any more, can't you see that? You were away too long, Marnie. His love for you died, you killed it by your own selfishness.' She spoke forcefully, but not in anger, if anything her voice was sad.

Marnie rounded on her furiously. 'And do you really think that he loves you?' She laughed jeeringly. 'Well, he doesn't! He didn't even look at you once he'd met me. He fell in love with me then and he always will.'

Her sister flinched, but said steadily, 'No, I don't think he does love me, but I love him—I always have.

And I can give him what he wants: a home, companionship and ... and ...' She lifted her head suddenly, defiantly. 'And I'm going to give him a child!'

For a long moment Marnie couldn't take it in, then she said stammeringly, as if there was something stuck in her throat, 'You're—you're going to have a baby? It's not true. I don't believe it!' But one look at their faces told her it was. Sue put a possessive hand on Alan's arm and he raised his other hand to cover it.

Somehow that gesture was the last straw, convincing Marnie as nothing else could that her sister had taken the man she had looked on as her future husband for so long. It was the first time in her life that she'd ever been hurt and her one desire was to hit back—hard. Shaking with rage, she yelled at Sue, 'You slut! You dirty slut! You did this deliberately. Tricked him into it because you knew it was the only way you'd ever get a man.' She rounded on Alan. 'And you. How could you do it? Can't you see how you've been used?' And then, out of her hurt and misery, hating them both, she said contemptuously, 'Well, I hope you'll both be very happy—you deserve each other! And just think what your offspring will be like—sly, spineless and doubly deceitful!'

She took a last look at them; Sue openly crying, and Alan's face chalk white, then she turned and ran out of the room before they could see the tears of hurt and unhappiness that came into her own eyes. Blindly she ran out into the hall, hearing her father call her name but taking no notice. Her car keys were lying on the dresser and she snatched them up and ran to the front door, fumbling with the catch and leaving it standing open behind her. Her car still stood in the driveway

where she had left it and somehow she managed to
find the right key and put it in the ignition. Her father
appeared in the doorway with the others behind him.
'No, Marnie! Stop!' But she started the car and
reversed it with a roar. Someone pulled open the passenger door and jumped in in the few seconds it took
her to change gear. It was Sue.

Breathlessly she said, 'Marnie, don't be an idiot.
Running away isn't going to solve anything.'

'Shut up! I don't want to talk to you.'

Marnie gunned the car forward and through the
gateway, her eyes still blurred by tears. Sue grabbed
hold of the door handle with no time to put on the
safety strap. It was very cold, but Marnie was so angry
that she didn't feel it. Sue was pleading with her to
stop, to go back, but she didn't take any notice. She
accelerated down the dark, narrow lane, the frost glistening like millions of tiny diamonds in the headlights,
and when the car coming fast down the road towards
them skidded on a patch of ice on a bend and came
directly at her, she had only time to try to swing the
wheel hard over before the car hit them, the impact
sending waves of sound to join the Christmas bells that
rang through the still air.

She hadn't passed out, that blessing hadn't been
granted to her. She had to sit in the car while it lay on
its side, the driver's side, and the firemen cut them
out. Just be there while her sister's life-blood dripped
on to her, her face and body a mangled mess. Lie there
knowing that if she had just turned the wheel it would
be her who had died and not Sue.

They had taken her to hospital suffering from shock,
but physically she was perfectly all right, not even
scratched. The police had come to reassure her; she

wasn't to blame for the accident; the other driver had been drinking nearly all day, was on his way from one party to another. Her father, too, had come, but he had looked suddenly old and crumpled and was unable to look her in the eyes any more. She had gone to the funeral, had somehow forced herself to go, and had faced the people who had either looked at her with horror or had turned their backs, but it had been Alan who had inflicted the final wound when he accused her of deliberately killing Sue.

She had gone back to London and tried to work, but had collapsed soon after and been taken to hospital again. A total nervous breakdown, the doctors called it, and gave her psychiatric treatment, keeping her in hospital for several weeks. During that time she had no visits from either Alan or her family, although she knew that the hospital had informed them that she was a patient. Eventually they let her out, physically able to cope, mentally still raw and bleeding, but better able to hide it now under a veneer of icy reserve. Immediately Marnie had got out of hospital she had sold everything she owned: clothes, jewellery, furniture, and with the proceeds, the insurance money for her car, which had been fairly new, and the money she'd saved towards her marriage, she had rented the cottage at Taornish for a year, with enough left over to keep her in food for that time. For somehow she knew that she just had to get completely away from the world she'd known, that only in peace and seclusion could she hope to find sanity again. So she'd come here with only the bare essentials of clothes, slipped quietly away without telling anyone, Alan, her family, or her friends, where she was going.

Marnie stirred at last; she had been sitting here for

so long that the tide had turned and was coming in
again. If she didn't move soon she would be cut off.
Already her limbs felt numb, her hands and feet frozen.
It took a great effort to move; it would have been so
much easier to just sit there and let the cold take over
until she couldn't feel anything any more, not in body
or in mind, but she forced herself to climb stiffly down
and walk back along the track to her cottage. As she
came near the neighbouring house her steps quickened,
but there was no sign of either the man or his dog. As
she passed the gate, Marnie noticed something carved
in its thick wood: 'SEANACHAIDH'—Gaelic, obviously, but she couldn't even pronounce it, let alone
guess what it meant.

The cottage felt very cold, but outside, at the back,
she found a brick-built store which housed the electricity generator and a spare drum of fuel to feed it,
together with a neat pile of sawn wood and several
stacks of dried peats. There was also an outhouse which
looked as if it might have been used as some sort of
dairy, with shelves and a long stone workbench, and
there was also a wooden lean-to built on to the back of
the store, but this had obviously not been used for
some time as several of the planks forming the walls
had come loose or broken. The wall surrounding the
cottage stretched for quite some distance and protected
land that had been used for both crops and small animals as part of the ground was wired off from the rest.
Perhaps someone had once kept hens when the cottage
was lived in all the time, but now that it was only let to
holidaymakers, for short periods usually, the coops had
been taken away.

Marnie collected an armful of the sawn wood and
raked out the ashes of the dead fire. Never having had

to light a fire before, she found it rather difficult at first, and used up several matches before she got it going, but eventually small yellow flames licked up the pieces of timber to give out a glow of warmth. Pleased with her success, she chose a boil-in-the-bag meal out of the freezer and when it had cooked, took it to eat in front of the fire, but was perturbed to see that it had already burnt quite low. Hurriedly she went outside and brought in some peats, putting four of them on to the fire. The pieces of wood underneath immediately collapsed under the weight and the fire went out. Resignedly Marnie started all over again. When the same thing happened a second time she swore violently and threw the poker back in the fireplace. Hell, she couldn't even keep a fire alight! Angrily she picked up her meal, but the food was cold and congealed on the plate. She buried her face in her hands, cursing herself for a fool, for having come to the place, and very close to giving way to tears.

Then the sound of someone whistling reached her and she lifted her head to listen. Quickly she got up and looked out of the window. It was the man from the house with the unpronounceable name, but without his dog this time. He was walking casually down the road towards her cottage with what looked like a wine bottle tucked under his arm, his head lifted as he watched some birds go swooping past. She had only seen him before in the dark or at some distance and now she found herself studying him more closely. There was something about the man that held her eyes, although there was nothing remarkable in the way he was dressed; he wore jeans, a thick Arran knit sweater with a dark jacket like a seaman's thrown loosely over it. He was probably in his early thirties and quite good-looking, she supposed, in a hard, lean sort of way, with grey eyes set below dark, level brows, high cheek bones and a strong, square jaw. He was tall, too, and correspondingly broad, but he moved with the grace and control of a powerful animal, as if he got plenty of exercise and was in the peak of physical condition. Perhaps it was the air of toughness about him that held her eyes, an aura of unshakeable confidence in his own strength and self-sufficiency. There was certainly something compelling about him, magnetic even.

With a start, Marnie realised that he had paused at the gate, had pushed it open and was coming up the path. Hastily she drew back and rushed to the door to make sure it was locked, then ran to the staircase even as she heard his knock echo through the little house. In her bedroom she hurried to the window again, but the dormer was set back in the roof and she couldn't see. She waited in an agony of suspense and presently the knocking came again, louder now. Drat the man, why wouldn't he go away? But presently he did, walking casually up the path and seeming to deliberately look up at her window as he paused to close the gate. Impossible for him to have seen her through the thick net curtains, of course, but she had the uncanny feeling that he knew darn well that she was watching him.

Later that afternoon Marnie managed to get the fire going, but only by using the wood; she couldn't get the peat to burn no matter how she tried, and only wasted a lot of the wood in the process. At this rate the pile of timber wouldn't last long at all, and she couldn't afford to buy any more. Then she remembered the lumps of coal and pieces of wood that she'd seen on the beach. Tomorrow she would pick some of them up and bring them back; it was too late today, it was already growing dark, much earlier than it had in London. It was time to draw the curtains, build up the fire, put on the lights and try and read herself into a torporific state so she would be too tired to think before the sleeping pills took effect.

Marnie woke late the next day and just lay in bed for a long time because it was so much warmer and there was nothing to get up for anyway. But at length she remembered the wood and thought that if she didn't go and get it the tide might have turned and floated it away again. But even then she didn't hurry, lethargically brushing her hair in front of the mirror and thinking how strange she looked without make-up. She had always had to wear so much before; the zany, way-out clothes that had been the fashion in recent years had called for extravagant, colourful make-up that had often taken hours to apply, especially for a photo session, and it had sometimes been a relief to model simpler clothes, but even then you had to wear quite heavy make-up to withstand the heat of studio lights or catwalk floodlighting. The face that stared back at her now, so pale and dark-smudged round her eyes, was that of a stranger—or a ghost, she thought drearily.

The wind had died down even more today, was not much more than a strong breeze, and the day was brighter, almost fair. There was no sign of the man who had called yesterday; she had made sure of that before she ventured out, but she hurried past his house anyway. She wondered fleetingly whether he lived there alone, but surely his wife would have called if he'd been married? Then she got annoyed with herself; what the hell did it matter whether he was married or not, just so long as he and everyone else in Taornish left her alone?

As she came out between the rocks at the start of the beach Marnie stopped in surprise. There was a large motor-cruiser moored in the bay, a beautiful white boat with sleek lines, bobbing gently at anchor, and drawn up on the shore was a dinghy which obviously came from the empty davits at the back of the cruiser.

Marnie hesitated, poised to turn and run back to the cottage, but there was no one on the shore and the boat looked deserted, its curtains drawn and the canopy closed. Slowly she walked towards the dinghy. It had a name painted on the side, but it was in Gaelic again and didn't mean a thing. She could just make out the same name on the side of the larger boat. She supposed that the boat must belong to her neighbour, Ewan McNeill, and wondered uneasily if he used the bay to moor his boat all the time. It would be a pity if she couldn't walk here any more; somehow the mood of the place fitted in exactly with the way she felt right now, grey and lonely, cold and empty.

There were several pieces of driftwood lying above the tideline and Marnie spent an hour or so dragging them along the beach to the start of the track and gathering them together in a pile. She was so weak that even this minor exertion had left her feeling exhausted and she had to stop and rest for a while before starting back to the cottage. She picked up some of the smaller pieces, wishing that she'd thought to bring some string to tie them into a bundle. The larger logs would have to wait until she could come back with a saw and cut them into manageable sizes.

She walked slowly back along the track towards the rocks, finding her load heavier than she'd expected, her nostrils filled with the tang of sea and salt. Then another aroma reached her and she looked up and came to a sudden stop. The McNeill man was sitting casually on a convenient piece of rock smoking a cigarette, just where the road narrowed between the two high walls of rock. His dog sat at his feet, ears pricked, watching her, ready to dart forward at any second. There was no way round them, they completely blocked the narrow road. Marnie stood still for a long moment wondering whether to turn back and wait for him to go away, but he looked as if he might sit there for ages. Hesitantly she moved forward again and the man turned to look at her. Marnie knew then, intuitively, that he had known she was here and had deliberately placed himself where she would have to pass him. A wave of impotent anger filled her and she walked forward more decisively.

'Good morning.' He got to his feet as she came up and placed himself squarely in front of her.

Marnie nodded curtly, not looking at him, and went to move on past him, but the dog was in the way.

'My name's Ewan McNeill. I live at Seanachaidh, the house in between yours and the sea.'

She nodded again, her face averted, willing him to move out of the way.

But instead he flicked the cigarette away and said, 'That bundle looks heavy; let me carry it back to your cottage for you.'

He made a move to take it from her, but Marnie backed away. 'I can manage, thanks,' she answered shortly. 'Would you please call your dog out of the way so I can get past?'

But he chose to ignore her, saying casually, 'I called on you yesterday to introduce myself and bring a bottle of wine. It's the custom on the island, you see, to greet

any stranger who settles in the neighbourhood with a
small gift of food or drink.' He paused a moment, but
when she didn't speak or look at him, went on, 'I
understand that Morag Ferguson made you such a gift
the day you arrived, but you made her take it back
again. She said you seemed very upset and was afraid
she'd offended you in some way. So she asked me to
explain about the custom and apolo . . .'

'All right, so now you've explained,' Marnie broke
in rudely, her arms aching unbearably, and longing to
escape. 'So will you please get out of my way?'

He stiffened, his face hardening. 'Now just a minute,
lady, you at least owe . . .'

But Marnie couldn't hold the logs any longer and
had to let them go. They crashed down on to the road
at her feet, making the dog jump back out of the way.

'Oh, hell!' Marnie looked down at the logs helplessly,
very close to tears. Then she turned furiously on Ewan
McNeill. 'Damn you! Get out of my way!' She thrust
at him violently and he automatically took a step backwards, more in surprise than anything else, and then
Marnie was past and running down the road as fast as
she could towards the sanctuary of her cottage.

Behind her she heard a shout of 'Wait!' but took no
notice and ran on, then the dog began to bark excitedly
and for a few terrible moments she thought that he
had sent it after her, but his command of 'Quiet!'
immediately silenced the animal and it was only her
own footsteps that echoed along the road, her own
panting breath that filled her ears. Once inside, she
slammed the door and leant against it, gasping for
breath, her heart hammering in her chest. Somehow
she managed to turn the key in the lock and then collapsed on to the settee, fighting to get her breath back.

God, she hadn't run so far or so fast in years!

Gradually her heaving chest stilled and she began to think over what had happened. If only he hadn't been there, waiting like that. Now she wouldn't dare to go to the beach to collect the rest of the wood she'd gathered in case he was waiting to waylay her again. Oh, damn the man, what did she care if Morag Ferguson or anyone else was upset? All she wanted was to be left in peace, and she'd been so sure she would find it here, but now even the solitude of the bay was denied to her. He must go there often if he kept his boat moored there and she was extremely loth to risk running into him again.

Listlessly she got up and began to open a couple of tins to make herself a meal, leaving the hotplates on to keep the kitchen warm while she ate. Half an hour or so later Marnie thought she heard a noise by the front door, but when she looked through the window saw only the tail of a Land Rover disappearing in the direction of the village. She remembered now catching a glimpse of the vehicle, parked at the side of McNeill's house when she had run past. She wondered how long he would be away. If he had taken a car it was quite likely that he was at least going to Ardsay, which would give her time enough to run back up the road and bring back the wood she'd dropped. She stood there for several minutes, indecisively, then decided suddenly to go and rushed to put on her coat and boots. Still pulling on her scarf, Marnie opened the front door and then stood staring. In a neat pile, sawn to a convenient size, were not only the logs she'd been carrying, but also the larger pieces which she'd gathered and left on the beach. For a moment her brain refused to function, then she remembered the noise she'd heard and realised that the McNeill man must have brought them down in his Land Rover and stacked them while she was eating.

Marnie continued to stare at the logs for several minutes before slamming the door shut again. If he thought that he was doing her a favour by bringing the wood, he was sadly mistaken. It could lie there and rot before she'd use a stick of it! She was quite capable of collecting her own fuel, thank you very much, and didn't need help from him or anyone else.

For the next two days Marnie kept the fire in the sitting-room fed with the wood stacked outside in the shed. It poured with rain both days, so there was no temptation to go out and she spent the time mostly reading. The bookcase beside the chimney contained quite a cross-section of books: modern novels as well as several copies of more classical works, children's stories, and quite a lot of non-fiction books on fishing and sailing, as well as half a dozen books on the Western Isles including the Outer Hebrides. Marnie glanced at these, but could work up no enthusiasm for them; she didn't want to know about the islands or be a part of them, she wanted to lose herself here, that was all. So she chose a copy of Tolkien's *Lord of the Rings* and was soon absorbed in a fantasy world that was a million times better than the real one.

But by the third day her stacks of wood were almost gone and she decided she'd have to try the peats again. This time she tried to be more scientific, but still the wretched things wouldn't burn. In desperation she got some of the diesel fuel from the shed and poured that on the fire. Nothing happened for a moment as Marnie stared at the peat disconsolately, then there was an almighty whoosh and a sheet of flames shot up the chimney. Clouds of soot and smoke belched out of the fireplace, covering her with black smuts. Marnie began to cough and put her arm up to protect her face. Picking up the poker she tried to hook the peats out on to the hearth, but this only seemed to make things worse as more smoke belched into the room. A great, continuous roaring noise came from the chimney and pieces of burning soot fell back into the fire. Oh, no, she must have set the chimney alight! Coughing, her eyes running, Marnie groped for the front door, unlocked it and stumbled out into the rain, smoke pouring out behind her as the wind gusted in and fanned the flames.

Eyes smarting, she looked up and saw bright yellow flames spouting out of the top of the chimneypot. God, what on earth was she going to do? She stared up at it helplessly for a moment, then realised she'd have to go back in. Water—she must put water on it and put out the fire.

She started for the front door again, her hand clasped over her nose and mouth, when running footsteps sounded behind her and she was pulled roughly aside.

'Keep out of the way. I'll handle it.'

McNeill hardly gave her a glance as he rushed into the house and began to deal with the fire. The smoke forgotten, Marnie ran in after him. He was deadening the flame by piling more peats on to it. Now, why hadn't she thought of that?

'*Do you mind?* I can manage perfectly well,' she began indignantly, then began to cough.

He stood up, an exasperated expression on his face, caught hold of her arm and shoved her out of the door again. 'Now stay out!' he ordered shortly.

Marnie's eyes opened wide in indignation. Of all the

nerve! She turned to angrily push past him and go inside, but saw the look on his face and stopped short. There was a distinct challenge there, a thrust of his jaw that said distinctly, 'Just try it.' And even in her anger she didn't have the strength to outrightly defy him, so she just glared at him malevolently but stayed where she was while he went back in and the smoke cleared and flames no longer belched out of the chimney.

'Okay, you can come in now.'

Slowly Marnie walked into the living-room, her hair damp and hanging limp. McNeill was standing by the now dead fire looking grimly at the jug she'd used to carry the diesel fuel. There was a dirty mark on his cheek and dark smudges of soot on his white polo-necked sweater, but the fire was dead and there was only a layer of grime over the room to tell of the near-disaster.

'I suppose you couldn't get the fire to draw and decided to help it along with this?' he said, indicating the jug. 'Why didn't you use the driftwood you brought up from the beach?'

'I didn't bring it up—you did,' Marnie pointed out tersely.

A frown came into his eyes. 'Look, Miss Adams, I don't know what you've got against . . .'

'How did you know my name?' she broke in.

'Morag Ferguson told me, of course,' he replied, his left eyebrow rising in surprise.

'Did she? In that case, while she was gossiping, she probably also told you that I didn't want her to come here again. Well, the same goes for you, Mr McNeill. I could have managed to put the fire out perfectly well by myself if you hadn't barged in.'

'Could you, indeed? I doubt it. You'd probably have run back and forward with ineffective pans of water which, even if they'd eventually managed to damp the fire, would have made the place in a bigger mess than it's in already.'

That this was exactly what she would have done only served to increase Marnie's anger. Nastily she said, 'Now that you've done your brave Boy Scout act, would you please leave?'

Ewan McNeill glanced at her for a moment, his dark brows drawn into a frown, and looked as if he was about to say something equally cutting, but instead he half-lifted a hand towards her and said, 'Look, I don't know what it is you've got against people trying to be helpful, but you can't live in a remote community like this without being to a large extent dependent on your neighbours. We rely on each other and you'll have to as well, if you want to survive. You wouldn't even let Morag show you how to lay a peat fire and look what happened.' He gestured towards the fireplace. 'There's an art to it. You have to make sure the peats are stacked so that . . .'

'I don't want to know,' Marnie interrupted forcefully. 'Not how to use the peat or anything else. I don't *need* help, do you hear me? I just want to be left alone.' Her voice had risen and there was a wild look in the deep blue of her eyes. 'Just keep away from me!' she shouted at him.

For a long moment her words hung in the air as McNeill stared into Marnie's face. Then he deliberately set down the jug and walked towards the doorway. On the threshold he paused and looked back. 'Okay, lady, have it your way,' he said coldly. 'But when you finally get round to learning some sense you'll know where to find me.' His mouth twisted wryly. 'Or else I'll be happy to provide transport to take you to Ardsay to catch the boat back to England. Because you sure as hell aren't going to last long on Culla the way you're going on.' Then he gave her a derisory nod and walked briskly away.

CHAPTER THREE

MARNIE was left alone in the cold room, the furniture and curtains soot and smoke-blackened and the floor and carpet wet where the rain had blown in through the open doorway. Her hair was wet and she was shivering with cold. She sat down on the settee feeling utterly dejected. It had been crazy to come to a place as far north as this when there wasn't even central heating in the house. She must have been mad to do it. The only sensible thing to do was to pack her things and to leave now, go abroad to Spain or somewhere where there would be warmth and sun. She stood up and ran upstairs to the bedroom, pulled her case down from the top of the wardrobe and began to fling things into it. There was the problem of money, of course, but she'd been here less than a week; surely the factor would give her back most of the three months' rent she'd paid in advance? She'd call in and see him on the way. And she would have to get a car to take her down to the pier to catch ... Marnie's feverish thoughts came to a sudden halt: what was it that odious McNeill man had said? That he'd be happy to provide transport for her when she gave up.

Marnie sank down slowly on the bed. Was she really going to give up so easily? After only a week? Have that insufferable man laugh when he saw her go, and say I told you so? She looked round the untidy room, the clothes she'd taken off just where she'd dropped them, the bed unmade because who was going to see it other than herself. The rest of the house, too, was in the same state; she hadn't bothered to wash any dishes after she'd used them, just shoved them in the sink and taken clean utensils from the cupboard. And it had all been so clean and neat when she'd moved in such a short time ago. But she had felt so listless for ages, as if all her strength and energy had been sapped away, and what point was there in taking care of the cottage or—she looked up and saw her reflection in the mirrors over the dressing table—or of herself? She leaned forward, studying herself in the mirror, really taking stock of her appearance for the first time in weeks. The honey-blonde hair that she had taken such care of, that used to be the first thing everyone noticed about her, now hung damply down to her shoulders. Picking up a towel, she dried it off, but even then it still looked lank and lustreless, a far cry from the silken glory it once had been. She hadn't bothered to wash it since she'd arrived here, hadn't bothered with anything, in fact. She had just sunk into a state of dejected apathy in which nothing mattered. But then no one cared about her, so why the hell should she care about herself? Her head bent and her eyes fell on her hands. They, too, were neglected, grimed with dirt where she'd been carrying the peat, the nails chipped and broken. Her nose wrinkled with distaste: and they smelt of some of the diesel oil that had spilt on them.

Well, even if there wasn't any heat in the house, there was at least plenty of hot water. Marnie washed her hair and then lay soaking in the bath until the water started to cool. It was the first time she'd felt warm all over for days.

The rest of the day she spent cleaning up the house, labouring over it as she'd never done over her London flat. It took ages to clear of all the smoke and soot in the living-room, but when she'd finished she looked around her with some satisfaction, tired but pleased that she'd made the effort. All the place needed really was some form of heating other than peat fires and it would be okay.

As she stood in the middle of the once again tidy room, a fire of blazing wood logs in the burnished grate, Marnie decided suddenly that she wasn't going to run away yet again, she would stick it out at Taornish for a month at least. This morning had been bad, very bad, but somehow she felt better now, more able to cope with things. A spark came to her blue eyes. And it would give her a great deal of satisfaction to show that insufferable Ewan McNeill that she could manage without help, his or anyone else's.

The next morning Marnie left the cottage early and turned left down the road, walking rather selfconsciously between the few crofts that formed the hamlet of Taornish, perfectly aware that there must be several pairs of eyes watching her from behind the net curtains. But she determinedly kept her head up and looked straight ahead until the narrow, rutted road ended at the junction with the main road to Ardsay. Hesitantly she looked to left and right, but there was no sign of a bus stop anywhere, so she turned towards Ardsay and began to walk, expecting to come across one with every turn in the road. The day had begun with a heavy pall of mist that lay low over the hills, but presently a fresh breeze came along to lift the mist and drive it away across the Atlantic, leaving the hills to glisten like sparkling granite in the first weak sunshine that Marnie had seen since she left England. The grass was very green and stretched away in a gradual incline to the foot of the hills. There were sheep on the lower pastures, white with black faces, and overhead the eternal gulls rose and screamed, the sun glistening on their fragile wings.

A postman passed her, cycling on his way to Taornish, and called out a greeting to which she replied with a nod, but apart from that there seemed to be very few people around, only a few men in the fields. Marnie must have walked for nearly a mile when she heard the sound of an engine behind her and turned to see an old, noisy, single-decker bus. Hesitantly she held out her hand, not sure what you were supposed to do to stop it. She hadn't ridden on a bus for ages, and then it had been the familiar red double-decker buses that were so much a part of the London scene. But the bus pulled up alongside her, its engine choking and wheezing, and she climbed inside. The driver charged her twenty pence to Ardsay, and she found a seat half-way down, flushing under the scrutiny of every other passenger, a few men, but mostly women, several of them with young children.

There had been a long moment of silence while they had all looked her over, but Marnie was used to that, her beauty had that effect on people who had never seen her before, but this silence was different, it had the quality of natives seeing a foreigner and the mental summing up process that entailed. But presently a child asked a question in a piping voice and, as if at a signal, everyone began to talk again. In Gaelic, of course, which she didn't understand, but it didn't take much guessing to know that they were discussing her quite freely.

Everyone got off at Ardsay and Marnie strolled down to watch the local fishing boats landing their catch. They were quite small boats with often only two, or at the most three men, to man them, and each seemed to have only one net which they stretched out along the jetty to dry, weighted down with empty oil drums at each end. The smell of sea and fish was very strong, the bright bodies of the captured fish tumbling in a vivid stream from the nets into baskets to be carried into a nearby shed to be cleaned and frozen. There seemed to be several different kinds of fish, one or two Marnie thought she recognised: herring and plaice, but the rest were completely unknown to her. And over everything there were the raucous cries of the seabirds as they wheeled above the boats, ready to dive for any scraps that were thrown over the side or even for a whole fish that might fall from one of the baskets and be fought over until every last piece was swallowed down their ever-hungry gullets.

There was quite a lot of activity down on the pier because the mail-boat was due in today and for a while Marnie watched that too, fascinated by a facet of life that was entirely new to her, but presently it began to rain again and she made her way back into the town. Marnie found a small café open where she treated herself to a meal, although it was rather expensive, then she wandered round looking in the shop windows and buying a few necessities, the hood of her anorak up against the rain. Eventually she found a shop selling electrical goods and bought a portable electric fire, the shop assistant taking his time over putting a plug on it for her as he tried to chat her up. Marnie rebuffed him coldly and made her way back to the point where everyone had got off the bus. She hung around for about ten minutes or so, but then a woman came up to her and asked her, 'Is it for the bus you're waiting now?'

'Yes, to Taornish,' Marnie nodded.

The woman shook her head sadly. '*A chruither*, I thought so. But the bus has gone, lassie, and there'll no' be another until six o'clock.'

Marnie thanked the woman in some dismay. There was nearly three hours to wait until six. And she had completely exhausted all the sights of Ardsay, there was just nothing left to see or do. Resignedly she picked up the electric fire in its box and began to walk. She supposed she could have taken a taxi, if she could find one, but it had been an expensive day and she didn't want to add to it. Living in the Outer Hebrides was expensive when nearly all the food and vegetables had to be brought over by boat.

There were quite a lot of people in the town, but once she had left the last of the houses behind the road stretched ahead of her, long, straight and deserted. Marnie plodded along in steadily worsening rain for half a mile or so, walking in the middle of the road to avoid the puddles on either edge, but moving over to the side when she heard a car coming up behind her. It was already quite dark and the car had its headlights on, so she had to put up a hand to shield her eyes when it drew up alongside her. The driver wound down his window and called out something in Gaelic.

Marnie took down her hand and shook her head. 'I'm sorry, I don't understand,' raising her voice to carry over the noise of the rain and the engine.

There was an exclamation and then the passenger door was pushed open and she could see the driver as he leaned across. It was the McNeill man. Impatiently he said, 'Don't just stand there in the rain, woman. Get in.'

A tight look came over Marnie's face. 'Thanks, but

I'd rather walk.' She pushed the door shut, hefted her parcel again and began to walk on.

The Land Rover started up, drove a couple of yards in front of her and came to a sharp stop. The driver's door slammed and Ewan McNeill strode purposefully towards her, shoulders hunched, an angry light in his eyes. Reaching out, he took hold of her parcel and wrested it easily from her grasp.

'Now wait a minute!' Marnie protested indignantly, but he calmly opened the back of the Land Rover and tossed the parcel inside. Then he turned towards her again. .

'You are about the most pigheaded woman I've ever had the misfortune to meet,' he told her bluntly. 'Are you going to get in the car or do I have to put you in there?'

'No, I am not,' Marnie retorted angrily. 'I've already told you that . . . Oh!'

She gave a startled exclamation of surprise as McNeill said, 'Right,' stooped down to put an arm round her hips and hefted her easily over his shoulder in a fireman's lift.

'Oh!' Marnie cried out again, unable to struggle in his iron grip, and desperately holding on to her bag and her other shopping. The next minute he had opened the passenger door and dumped her in the seat anyhow. By the time Marnie had gathered her wits and her belongings he was back in the driving seat and they were moving.

She rounded on him furiously. 'How *dare* you! Stop this car at once. Do you hear me?' she demanded when he took no notice of her.

He glanced at her laconically. 'Oh, sure, I hear you.'

'Then stop this car at once and let me out.'

'You'd really rather walk four miles in the rain?'

'Yes, I would,' she agreed angrily. 'If I'd wanted to ride I could have taken a taxi or waited for the bus. And I'd rather walk *ten* miles than ride anywhere with *you*,' she added forcefully.

To her increased annoyance, he laughed. 'Boy, are you something else! I don't know who the hell put that chip on your shoulder, but until you get rid of it you sure aren't going to be fun to live with.'

Marnie glared at him and said sarcastically, 'Well, that hardly need concern you, because I certainly wouldn't want to live with an obnoxious brute like you!'

McNeill looked across at her, a sardonic glint in his grey eyes. 'I wasn't asking you to,' he returned coolly.

Her mouth fell open and Marnie gaped at him for a moment. 'But that wasn't what I . . . I didn't . . .' She closed her mouth angrily and snapped out, 'Will you *please* stop the car and let me out?'

'No.'

'Well, if you won't, then I will.' Furiously she reached forward and across him to try and turn off the ignition key.

His left arm shot out and pushed her roughly back into her seat, held her there even though she tried with all her strength to push him away. 'You rotten pig! Let me go! How dare you treat me like this?' At length she had to give up, subsiding into the seat breathless and defeated. Only then did McNeill remove his arm.

'Lady,' he said tersely, 'why don't you just sit down and shut up?'

Marnie stared at him, for the second time bereft of words. *How dared he?* No one had ever used her so roughly or been so rude to her in her life! Especially men. They had always treated her like some fragile plant ever since she was a small child. Her father's favourite and hopelessly spoiled by him, she had been used to having her own way ever since she could remember. Even Alan, who could have exerted some influence over her when she was young and impressionable, had let her twist him round her little finger, giving way to her when she showed signs of petulance because she was so lovely when she smiled and so loving and grateful when she got what she wanted. And it had been the same in London; most of the men she met were happy to just act as her escort, although some, in the early days, had been more opportuning and difficult to get rid of, but in time she'd learnt how to recognise and handle these, her air of delicacy helping a great deal, and there was always her engagement ring to flash under their noses as a further put-off. Admittedly a few men had tried the masterful approach in an attempt to impress her and she had given them short shrift, but not even one of those had dared to handle her so roughly and tell her to sit down and shut up.

Marnie glared at McNeill morosely, his face shadowed by the gathering dusk, mentally swearing at him furiously, the surge of hatred she felt for him creating a tense atmosphere in the car. He must have felt it, it was impossible not to, but he gave no sign, didn't even look particularly annoyed. He was looking straight ahead, concentrating on the road through the rain-splashed windows, the wipers fanning back and forth with an interminable soft swishing sound.

Arms folded, Marnie sat back in her seat, stiff and tense, mouth closed into a stubborn line, looking fixedly out of the window into the darkening night and waiting impatiently for the journey to end. At last they pulled up outside her cottage and she reached eagerly for the door handle, but McNeill turned in his seat.

'Wait, I want to talk to you.'

'Well, I certainly don't want to listen,' Marnie retorted, and pushed down the door handle.

Immediately his hand gripped her arm, holding her fast. 'You're not going anywhere until we've talked.'

'You just now told me to shut up,' Marnie reminded him resentfully. 'Why don't you make up your mind? If you're capable of doing anything so difficult as making a decision, that is?' she added tauntingly.

A disgusted look flickered across his lean features. 'A cheap crack like that is more suited to a ten-year-old than a grown woman.'

With a rather sickening feeling of self-revulsion Marnie realised it was true, and she turned again to fumble with the door handle, a faint flush of colour in her cheeks.

The grip on her arm tightened, she could feel his fingers pressing into her flesh through the thickness of her clothes. 'I've told you I've got something to say to you,' he said curtly.

An angry sparkle in her eyes, Marnie answered tautly, 'Then will you please get on with it so that I can get out of this car?'

'All right!' His jaw thrust forward angrily. 'Morag asked me to speak to you again. I tried to explain to her that you were too eaten up by bitterness and spite to even behave like a rational human being, that you'd scornfully reject any overtures of friendship or even common civility. But she refused to believe that anybody could be that bloody-minded and she's asked me to invite you to her daughter's *reiteach* next Saturday night. She would have asked you herself, but she's afraid of offending you again.' Then he added force-fully, disgust again in his face, 'Do you understand what I'm saying? *She's* afraid of offending *you*?'

Marnie stiffened, angered by his insulting tone. 'What is a *reit* . . . that thing you said?' she asked coldly.

'A *reiteach*. It's a betrothal party. Morag's daughter, Katie, has got engaged to Hector Cameron from Ardsay. Everyone in Taornish is invited, including you. Will you come?'

'No.'

'Right.' He let go of her arm and sat back, looking ahead again, his hand already reaching for the ignition key. 'Don't forget to take your parcel out of the back.'

Marnie gazed at him, surprised by his action and lack of argument. She felt as if she ought to justify herself somehow and began awkwardly, 'Look, I . . .'

But he turned a cold, implacable face towards her and said curtly, 'You wanted to get out, lady, *now get*.'

For a brief second Marnie continued to stare into those hard grey eyes, then she grimly got out of the car and took the electric fire out of the back. He was away the moment she had slammed the door.

Conditions improved in the cottage with the help of the electric fire, and even more so when it occurred to Marnie that she could use the wood from the tum-bledown outhouse for the sitting-room fire. First she used the pieces that had fallen off, breaking them into smaller pieces with an axe, and when these were used up knocking down more of the planks that were hang-ing off the sides of the building. This way she was able to keep both the sitting-room and her bedroom warm and didn't lie shivering with cold between the sheets any more, surrounded by hot water bottles that only made small oases of warmth in the large, feather-mattressed bed.

She only walked down on the beach a couple of times, when she had seen McNeill drive past in his Land Rover and was sure that he was well out of the way, but even so she was reluctant to linger there, unable to appreciate the solitude of the place in case he came back and she met him again, either by accident or intent. So instead she took to walking in the rock-strewn moorland at the back of the house, strolling along paths that were little more than sheep tracks and stopping to watch a thin burn of crystal clear water tumbling down from the purple hills towards the sea, or sheep, one or two of them already with tiny lambs at their side. And always there were birds: stonechats with black heads and chestnut breasts, and wheatears, their white rumps flashing in the light, as well as the seabirds, terns, black and white oyster-catchers and flock upon flock of grey gulls.

There were few people out on the hills, just an occasional shepherd inspecting the ewes, but once she saw Morag Ferguson, a scarf tied round her hair and a brightly floral pinafore showing under her coat, standing with her wellingtoned feet in a reed-edged burn dunking a large pile of what looked like mustard-coloured matted wool in the water. Marnie watched for a moment, wondering what on earth the woman could be doing, but hurried on with averted head when Morag glanced up, afraid that the elder woman might try to speak to her.

On the night of the unpronounceable betrothal party, Marnie heard footsteps go past the house and guessed that McNeill was on his way there. Soon the sound of music coming from what she guessed was a piano, an accordion and a couple of fiddles from the tone of it, came creeping back up the road from a large barn-like building near the junction of the main road. When she went to bed she saw that the place was ablaze with light, the music continuing indefatigably, and later, around midnight, there was the sound of singing and drunken shouts as a lot of people made their way back to Mrs Ferguson's house about a hundred yards down the road.

Marnie smiled to herself in the darkness; they all seemed as if they'd celebrated the occasion by toasting the engaged couple as often as possible. She'd heard somewhere that most islanders were hard drinkers, and wondered fleetingly if the McNeill man was one of the singers staggering up the road. But at once, with instinctive certainty, she knew that he wasn't. He was the sort of man who would enjoy having a drink, probably a good few drinks, with his friends, but who would never let himself get out of control, of his senses or his emotions. He was tough, hard and insensitive, but completely self-disciplined.

That night was a bad one for Marnie. She lay awake, the sleeping pills for once having no effect, listening to the gradually diminishing noise of the party. She told herself fiercely that she was glad that she hadn't gone, would have been a fish out of water and would have hated every minute of it, as well as being the object of everyone's curiosity. And she was in no mood for parties and celebrations; she would have looked at the engaged couple and remembered that Alan had jilted her, thrown her aside for her plain elder sister. But even though she told herself all this over and over, a feeling of utter loneliness and despair filled her, the fear that she would never know love, happiness or even peace of mind ever again, and she turned her face into her pillow and wept long and bitterly.

April came in with icy gales that shook the house with their ferocity, the rain lashing fiercely against the windowpanes from black clouds that made the day almost as dark as night. Marnie listened to the radio, heard warnings of Force Eight winds in the area, and shivered, imagining how the sea would rage against the cliffs in the bay and glad that she wasn't a sailor in this weather. But the storms ceased as suddenly as they had come and seemed to have blown the last of winter away with them, for although it was still cold, there was a softening in the air, a slight hint that spring was not far away.

After being cooped up indoors for several days, it was a great relief for Marnie to be able to wrap herself up and go walking over the moors. She would have liked to have gone down to the bay, but thought that the McNeill man would probably have gone there to check on his boat. She had heard him go past the house several times in his Land Rover and had felt a pang of envy for his freedom of movement even in such foul weather.

She walked for a long time that first day, farther than she had ever walked before, high up into the hills where the black-faced sheep ran baaing out of her way as if she imposed some threat to the silly creatures. Out of breath, Marnie found a flattish rock and rested for a while, a glow of exertion in her cheeks and taking in great gulps of the fresh, sparkling clear air. The westerly tip of the island lay spread out before her, the jaggedly uneven line of the coast, ringed by white-capped waves of the incoming tide, the spaced out, grey-roofed houses on either side of the road, and everywhere the bright green of new grass. There were very few trees to be seen, especially here near the coast where they had to fight for survival against the strength of the eternal winds, just a few, their branches still bare, clustered in the lee of houses or walls. It looked a very peaceful place, hardly touched by the hand of man really, only the regularly spaced telegraph poles that marched alongside the roads giving a hint of the twentieth century.

Marnie walked back more slowly, stopping with an exclamation of delight when she saw some fragile yellow primroses growing in a cluster near a stream. She bent to look at them more closely, and as she did so another splash of colour caught her eye, red this time, and on a large, flat stone at the edge of the stream just out of the water. It looked as if someone had spilt red paint, and recently too because it looked still wet. Curiously Marnie took off her glove and reached out to touch it, wondering who on earth would want red paint out on the hillside. Perhaps the shepherds were marking the sheep or something. Her thoughts came to a sudden, startled stop as she looked at her finger and realised that it wasn't paint at all—it was blood!

She stood up and looked wildly round, not really knowing what she expected to see, but there was no one lying injured nearby, nothing to give her a clue to who had spilt the blood. For a minute she hesitated, wondering what to do, then decided to follow the stream down the hill to see if there were any more blood splashes. She walked slowly on, stooping down to examine the ground carefully and eventually finding more traces, but whether the injured person was going up or down stream she had no idea. After a quarter of a mile or so, Marnie thought she heard a noise and raised her head to listen. After a while it came again; a howling noise like a child crying. Perhaps one of the village children had been hurt and was too weak to get home. Immediately she broke into a run, stumbling over the uneven ground, afraid in case the sound stopped before she traced it. There were some boulders that had fallen into the stream, acting as a dam so that the water spread out into a boggy area. Marnie splashed heedlessly through the bog, rounded the boulders and stopped short in surprise. It wasn't a child she'd been following at all, it was a dog, a glossy chestnut Great Dane. McNeill's dog. It lay on the grass beside the stream, trying ineffectively to lick its front paw from which the blood was flowing freely, and howling plaintively.

Marnie gave a gasp of relief, the terrible visions that she'd imagined disappearing. But the dog still needed help. She moved closer to it rather gingerly; the only other times she'd seen the animal it had either growled or barked at her. It stopped licking its paw and lifted its head to look at her. Marnie reached a tentative hand out towards it and began to talk to it soothingly.

'There, there, nice dog. Good boy, then. Nobody's going to hurt you.'

Slowly she moved nearer, making sure that she made no sudden movement to startle the animal. It watched her warily, its body tense.

'Good boy. Hold still, then.'

Gently Marnie lowered her hand on to its head and began to stroke it. Slowly the dog relaxed and its tail moved, then it put out its long tongue and licked her wrist.

'Why, you're nothing but an old softy! That savage dog scene was just a big act.' She felt round his neck for a collar, but it was bare. Presumably McNeill didn't think it necessary for an identity disc when everyone on the island must know who the dog belonged to. But Marnie would have liked to have known his name.

After she'd petted the Dane for several minutes she gently lifted up his injured paw. 'Let's have a look, shall we?' Her stomach turned over a little at the sight of the cut, which went quite deeply into one of the pads of his paw. 'Now how on earth did you do that, you poor old boy? I think we'd better try and bathe it in the stream.'

With some difficulty she tugged the dog nearer the stream and washed the paw as best she could in the cold water, then used first her handkerchief and then a piece torn from her blouse to bind it up. But the dog would only take a few steps and the wound would be dirty again. She frowned, trying to think what to do. A memory came back to her suddenly of an autumn walk through a wood with Alan, the leaves bright bonfires of flame and gold. It was while he was still studying to become a vet and they had come across a cat with a cut paw. Alan had used a soft leather sunglasses case as a cover for the wound. Well, she didn't have anything like that, but she did have a glove. Marnie looked at them rather ruefully: they were fur-lined sheepskin mittens, bought just before she came to Culla, and beautifully warm. When she'd been without a fire she'd even worn them in the house. Still, the dog's need was greater than hers. She carefully slipped the Dane's fat paw into the mitten and pulled the drawstring out of the bottom of her anorak to tie it in place.

'There, that should hold until you get home. Come on, boy.'

Obediently the dog got to its feet, standing higher than her waist, and limped along beside her across the moors. Of necessity they went slowly, Marnie doing her best to find the softest path for him, and it was almost dusk when they at last reached Taornish. She walked with the dog to the gate of McNeill's house and was relieved to see that a light was on in one of the rooms at the front of the house; she had been afraid that he might have been away and she would have to try and get the dog to a vet herself, with all the difficulties that that entailed.

She knelt by the dog and stroked it. 'There you are, you'll be all right now. Go home, boy, go home.'

The dog whined a little and pulled at her sleeve with his teeth.

'No, you're on your own now. Go on, you sloppy old thing! Go find your master.' She stood up and gave him a push and the dog limped down the pathway. At the door it began to bark, and Marnie turned and ran down the road towards her cottage. Behind her she heard the door of McNeill's house open and then his voice as he spoke to the dog. Then he called out, 'Hey, there. Wait a minute!' but she ran on, confident that he wouldn't recognise her in the near darkness, and let herself into the house. Five minutes later the Land Rover roared past, heading towards Ardsay, presumably on the way to the nearest vet.

Marnie threw her one mitten on to a chair and took off her coat and scarf. She felt tired, cold and hungry, but somehow physically better than she'd felt for ages. It must have been the fresh air after having been cooped inside for so long.

The next morning Marnie decided it was time to replenish her store of wood, which had got very low during the gale, and she started knocking down some more of the shed. Raising her axe to chop the planks into pieces small enough to fit the grate, she swung the axe down wildly, missing the plank altogether as she caught sight of the McNeill man walking quite brazenly round the corner of her house.

She stared at him for a moment and then turned, tight-lipped, to vainly try to pull the axe out of the piece of log she was using as a chopping block.

'Good morning.'

Marnie ignored him and wrestled with the axe handle.

'I came over to thank you for what you did for Brutus yesterday.'

Gritting her teeth, Marnie tugged again at the axe, cursing the thing for being so obstinate. Then the McNeill man gently pushed her aside, gripped the axe handle, and with a jerk of his wrist freed it from the log. As easily as Arthur might have freed Excalibur from the stone. She waited, mouth set into a thin line, for him to either make some sarcastic comment or to start chopping the rest of the wood, as if she was incapable. To her surprise he did neither, just laying the axe down and standing back.

'I'm sorry about your glove—I'm afraid it was ruined. The wound had opened up again after you bound it up.'

Marnie lifted her head to look at him for the first time. He was wearing the usual well-cut jeans but with a dark blue sweater this time. It suited him. For a fleeting moment she wondered what he would look like in a dinner jacket with a crisp white shirt to show off his lean, tanned features. But that she'd even had such a thought made her angry and she said irascibly, 'Am I supposed to know what you're talking about?'

A slightly amused look came into his eyes. 'Oh, I'm quite sure you do, otherwise I wouldn't be here.'

'Well, nobody invited you, that's for sure.'

The amused look deepened so that his eyes crinkled up at the corners, and he leaned negligently against one of the corner posts of the old shed. 'Which is why I made a point of coming when you were in the garden and couldn't pretend you weren't in the house when I knocked.'

Marnie looked away, ready to be annoyed if he became sarcastic again, but quickly turned to look at him when he said warmly, 'I'm really very grateful, you know.'

There was sincerity in his voice and in his grey eyes and she flushed a little, embarrassed. 'How is he this morning?'

'Brutus? Oh, he's fine, thanks to you and the vet in Ardsay.'

'Is that his name? I didn't know: he wasn't wearing a collar. It doesn't suit him,' she said, smiling a little.

McNeill's eyes opened wider, a strange expression in them for a fleeting second. He seemed to catch his breath and his voice was slightly unsteady as he answered, 'So you found him out, did you?' He straightened up and the post creaked and moved a little. 'Did you see how he cut himself?'

Marnie shook her head. 'No, I happened to see a splash of blood on a stone by the stream and I followed the trail until I found him.'

'Which stream was that?'

She turned and pointed. 'Over there, at the back of the house.

'Unfortunately there are several streams on the hillside.' He looked at her speculatively. 'You don't think you could show it to me, do you?'

Immediately Marnie began to shake her head, 'Oh, no, I . . .'

'Because I'd hate the same kind of accident to happen again,' he went on smoothly, as if she hadn't spoken. 'Not only to Brutus, but to any of the animals that roam the hills: sheep, sheepdogs, rabbits.'

She hesitated. 'It might just have been a sharp stone or a piece of rock,' she pointed out.

He shook his head decisively. 'No, the cut was much too deep, and the flesh looked as if it had been sliced. I'm pretty sure it must have been a piece of glass or metal. And I'd like to find it before it does more damage, if you'll help me.' He looked at her enquiringly, one eyebrow slightly raised.

Marnie searched his face, looking for any hint of challenge or amusement, but there was none, only a slight frown of worry and concern. At last she nodded. 'All right, I'll come with you as far as the stream.'

'Thanks.' McNeill went to walk ahead of her, but then looked back. 'That corner post didn't feel too stable.' He glanced up at the corrugated iron roof with a frown and looked as if he was going to say something more, but saw the angry challenge in her eyes and left it at that.

They went round the side of the house and began to walk across the moors towards the hills. Marnie stuck her hands in the pockets of her jacket and walked along beside him, but keeping a distance between them, letting him know that this was only a temporary thing, that she still intended to remain aloof.

'How far up the hill did you find him?' he asked her.

She pursed her lips. 'I suppose it must have been nearly a mile away. How did the dog get out?'

'He's free to roam where he likes. He's been trained not to worry the sheep.'

'What about people?' she asked tartly.

McNeill turned to look at her. 'As you've found out, he's a very friendly dog. He wouldn't harm anyone unless he had a good reason.'

'He growled at me,' she pointed out.

'Ah, yes.' He looked at her enigmatically. 'But you were a stranger then.'

Marnie shot him a darkling glance, wanting to say that she was still a stranger, that she wanted to be nothing else, but somehow it seemed silly when she was walking with him across the moors. Instead she turned away and lengthened her stride, wanting to get it over.

They walked on in silence for a while, the McNeill man easily keeping pace with her and not even looking as if he was doing more than strolling. Marnie tried to concentrate on the scenery, but found it strangely difficult: she felt too on edge for some reason. More wild flowers were beginning to appear in the grass now and she carefully walked round a clump of yellow coltsfoot.

'Not much point in trying to avoid them,' McNeill remarked. 'Soon all the *machair* will be covered in wild flowers—when they're not being rooted up by tourists, that is,' he added wryly.

'*Machair?*' Marnie asked uncertainly.

'Sorry, that's the grassland here at the foot of the hills that reaches down to the shore.'

'Do you get many tourists?' Marnie had a sudden

vision of the place being overrun by holidaymakers.

'Quite a few in the summer. Some stay a week or so, but most of them come over by boat from Skye, spend the day here and then go back in the evening. One or two artists always seem to come every year and stay for the season. It's the light that attracts them; it has an intensity that seems to bring out the colours.' He paused for a moment, then added with a reassuring note, 'We're not too bothered by tourists up here in Taornish, although I have had them knocking on my door asking for bed and breakfast, or if my boat's for hire.'

'That's the cruiser I've seen in the bay?'

'Yes.' McNeill gave her a quick, considering look. 'Do you like boating?'

Marnie shrugged. 'I've only been a few times, and then only on the Thames. I've never been out to sea.'

'Perhaps you'd like to come out with me sometime,' McNeill said casually. 'You get an entirely different perspective of Culla from the sea. It looks as if it almost floats on the water.'

'No, thanks,' Marnie replied shortly. She stopped and pointed. 'The stream where I found Brutus is over there. I found him near a place where a rock has blocked the stream and made the ground boggy. And the first bloodstain I saw was about half a mile higher up near where a patch of primroses were growing.'

'Morning stars.'

She frowned. 'What?'

'The Hebrideans call primroses morning stars,' he explained. 'Don't you want to come up there with me and find out what cut Brutus?'

'No, I'm going back now.'

'Suit yourself.' He looked at her rather derisively.

'Don't read anything into the invitation to come out on the boat that isn't there. I often go out for a cruise round the island when the weather's fine. If you want to come along, okay. I don't give a damn either way. If all you want to do is sit alone and wallow in your self-pity then that's your privilege.'

Tightly Marnie replied, 'I do *not* wallow in self-pity.'

'No?' he replied tauntingly. 'Then just what would you call it when you shut yourself away and refuse to have anything to do with anyone? You're so sorry for yourself that you want to make everyone else miserable too.'

'That isn't true,' Marnie declared hotly. 'I just want to be left alone!'

'Then why not come right out and say it in an adult manner instead of putting everyone's backs up? No one wants to intrude on your privacy, but you don't have to be so damned bad-tempered about it.'

Marnie glared at him furiously. 'Oh, shut up! What the hell do you know about it?'

'So tell me.'

'Tell you?' Her look changed to one of contempt. 'Tell you and tell the whole of Culla!'

McNeill's jaw thrust forward angrily and he caught hold of her wrist. 'If you were a man I'd give you a punch on the nose for that!'

'So what's stopping you?' Marnie retorted jeeringly.

He gave a short laugh. 'Don't tempt me, lady.' His lip curled wryly. 'God, I pity the poor devil who drove you into shutting yourself away here. He must have gone through pure agony before he found the courage to tell you to get the hell out of his life.'

Marnie's face went very pale. 'I don't know what

you mean. My coming here had nothing to do with a man.'

'No?' His dark eyes ran over her face and then slowly down her body, undressing her. 'But I'm sure there is. You're far too desirable for there not to be a man in the background somewhere.'

Marnie stared at him, her face ashen. She had been mentally stripped by many men, but never quite like that. Usually it was done leeringly, the men imagining what they would like to do to her body. But McNeill's stripping was frank and open and not even appreciative. There had been no lust in his eyes, or even desire. It was merely an appraisal with which to confirm his surmise. Her lips parted in surprise, Marnie continued to gaze at him speechlessly. She was used to her beauty having a stunning effect on men, of bringing out the protective instinct in them, never of this complete immunity, this manner of treating her face and her figure as if they were something to be weighed up and rejected.

Anger swelled up inside her suddenly and she snatched her wrist away. 'And just what right do you think you've got to criticise me?' she demanded furiously. 'You live in this Godforsaken place too, remember? Just what makes you shut yourself away here? You're not a native: you neither look nor speak like one. So what are *you* running away from, McNeill? A woman? A situation you can't handle?' Her voice rose mockingly, echoing across the hillside. 'Or even from a man?'

His hands flashed out and grabbed her arms, jerking her towards him. Marnie smelt the tangy mixture of the sea and tobacco from his sweater in her nostrils for a moment before she lifted her head and saw the storm warnings in his eyes.

'And just what was that remark supposed to mean?' he demanded fiercely.

Marnie gazed up at him, taken aback by his vehemence and feeling suddenly frightened. 'I—I don't know,' she faltered. 'It was just—just something to say, I suppose.'

The grip on her arms relaxed a little, but he still looked angry. 'You crazy little idiot! Don't you ever stop to think before you start insulting people? When the hell are you going to grow up and learn to face the knocks that life gives you without trying to hit back at everybody else? You don't . . .'

'Oh, shut up!' Marnie interrupted, her nerve recovered and furious again. 'Stop moralising at me, for God's sake. Get off my back, McNeill!'

She pulled against his hold and he suddenly let her go so that she lost her balance and fell backwards on to the grass.

McNeill looked down at her sardonically. 'It'll be a pleasure, Adams. You've been nothing but a pain in the neck since you got here.' And then he turned and left her lying there while he continued on his way towards the stream.

Slowly Marnie picked herself up, rubbing her backside tenderly. That insufferable man; he'd intended that she should fall, and he hadn't even offered to give her a hand up. Not that she'd have taken it; help from him would be the last thing she'd take, but it would have been highly satisfactory to spurn his offer. Which was probably why he never made it, she realised resentfully. She gazed after his broad back as he climbed easily up the hillside, stepping out with long strides and making far better progress than when she'd been with him. God, how she hated the man! She'd only met him a few times and yet at each meeting something happened to increase her dislike of him.

Turning, she began to walk back down the hill. Of all the bad luck—to come to such an isolated spot in search of peace and quiet only to find someone as odious as McNeill on her doorstep. Why the hell couldn't the man mind his own business and leave her to mind hers? And such a belligerent man, too. Why, he'd almost shaken her back there, and that glint in his eyes had been definitely dangerous. She tried to remember what she'd said that had angered him so much. Something about running away, that was it. From a woman, or a set-up, or a man. Marnie blushed, realising how he must have interpreted her remark. But she hadn't meant that at all; she'd just blurted it out in the heat of the moment. It had never even entered her head that there might be anything even slightly bent about McNeill. He was far too arrogantly masculine for that, the male chauvinist in his prime. And he was definitely used to handling women. Marnie remembered the way he had mentally undressed her and her cheeks burned.

Her mind absorbed in her thoughts, she jumped over another stream and went on over the field. For the first time she wondered just how the McNeill man did earn his living. He must be pretty well off to have that large new house and the cabin cruiser, and yet he didn't seem to go out to work at all, coming and going at irregular times and often out with Brutus during the day. And he didn't *look* as if he did any work. Every time she'd seen him he'd been wearing jeans and a sweater.

From work it was an easy step to surmising about

the romantic side of his life. Did he have a woman in his past? she wondered. Perhaps he was divorced and had come to Culla to forget—and in considerably more comfort than joining the French Foreign Legion, Marnie thought with a wry smile. He was old enough for that to have happened, about thirty-two or three, she judged. Or perhaps—her thoughts froze—perhaps his wife had died, and he too had come here to try and conquer his grief. It was a romantic picture and Marnie dwelt on it for a while, elaborating it, but it suddenly came to her that McNeill wasn't that sort of man. However terrible he felt inside he would never be afraid to face up to reality, was tough enough to pick up the pieces and go on living. Not like her. For a long time she hadn't even been able to face up to waking up in the morning or going to sleep at night. But perhaps McNeill hadn't also been spurned by all the people in the world who meant anything to him.

But she mustn't think of that, not of herself. Concentrate on McNeill, think of him. Even thinking about a louse like him was better than remembering. He must have been here for some time, though, because he spoke Gaelic and seemed on good terms with the people in Taornish, even knowing their customs and being invited to their houses. Perhaps he had come here as a holidaymaker, fallen in love with the place, and stayed, but he had spoken knowledgeably about the tourists in an 'us and them' way, as if he wasn't and never had been anything but an islander. Marnie frowned in perplexity. The McNeill man seemed to be something of an enigma. If she had been in the mood to care about anyone she might have been curious about him, but right now she just wished he'd get out of her life and stay out.

CHAPTER FOUR

FOR two days the weather stayed fine and sunny, the wind dropped and it was almost as warm as an English spring day. McNeill seemed to have taken advantage of the weather to go cruising, because his boat wasn't in the bay when Marnie went for a walk there. It was as deserted as she'd first seen it, but the sea was more gentle now and she saw what McNeill had meant by the quality of the light; it was pure and brilliant and made everything look so vivid and clean, the sky a breathtaking blue, the green of the *machair* a rich emerald. She spent several pleasant hours in the bay, exploring rock pools, and picking among the seaweed for shells, but the next day she bypassed the bay and walked along the headland parallel to it, gradually climbing until she reached the high cliffs that fell sharp and steep down to the rock-strewn sea below. From here the horizon stretched for miles, and looking out to sea Marnie could just make out the rocky outline of another, much smaller island out farther to the west.

She walked along the cliffs for a mile or so before turning back, enjoying the sun on her back and the peace and tranquillity of the landscape. As she neared the bay again, Marnie glanced out to sea and saw a small boat, the sunlight reflected on its white paint, turn and head for the entrance. She couldn't be sure from this distance, but it looked like McNeill's boat. He brought it in through the mouth of the bay and swung it with practised hand broadside on to the beach before cutting the engines and letting go the anchors. Marnie stood and watched him for a while, again wondering how he came to be on Culla. He was much nearer now and she could see him as he moved about the deck, coiling ropes and generally clearing up after his voyage. It came to her that he was a very capable man, able to handle himself in any sort of situation, however difficult. The right sort of person to have around if you were ever in trouble.

Almost as if he had sensed her regard, McNeill looked up in her direction and saw her standing on the cliff top. He lifted a casual hand in greeting and continued to watch her.

Marnie looked down at him indignantly; he didn't really expect her to wave back after he'd been so rude to her, did he? But evidently he did, for he was still looking up. Almost against her will, Marnie took her hand from her pocket and raised it in acknowledgment. Then she turned hastily, thrust her hand back in her jacket pocket, and walked on down the path, angry with herself for having relaxed her attitude of aloofness even that much. But there had been something in the way that McNeill had stood and watched her that had compelled her to wave to him. It was as if he had willed her to do it, and she lacked the power to resist.

But if Marnie was annoyed with herself then, she was even angrier when, later that evening, she heard the letterbox rattle and found two packages on the doormat. They were both wrapped in plain brown paper and Marnie looked at them for a long moment before stooping to pick them up. She guessed what the first one was even before she opened it and felt no surprise when she saw the pair of mittens it contained.

They were almost identical to her old ones, and when she slipped her hands inside their soft, fancy interiors, she found that they were exactly the right size. He must have taken her old one with him when he bought them. She frowned, wondering where McNeill had got them; she certainly hadn't seen any in the shops in Ardsay when she went there to buy the fire. Then she remembered that his boat had been gone for two days. Could that possibly mean that he had gone over to Skye or to the mainland to buy them? But surely no one would bother to go all that way just to replace a pair of gloves? She stared down at the mittens in disbelief, but the conviction gradually grew that it must be so. She had the idea that McNeill wasn't the kind of man who liked to be for long in anyone's debt, especially if that someone had behaved as belligerently towards him as she had.

Slowly Marnie took off the gloves and sat with them in her lap, her fingers idly smoothing the suede. Should she accept them or not? Her first instinct had been to march over to his house and throw them back in McNeill's face, tell him she wanted nothing from him. But it was obvious that he had been to some trouble to replace the originals as closely as he could, giving her back a pair that was neither cheaper nor more expensive. It came to her that if she had been in his place she would have done exactly the same thing for fear of offending him. And because he had taken so much care, the thought of throwing them back at him seemed somehow petty and smallminded. And besides, her hands had been very cold these last couple of days, despite the warmer weather. Picking up the mittens, she put them to one side, reserving judgment, and turned her attention on the other package.

It contained a book, a slim hardback, entitled *Natural Flora of the Hebrides*. With it was a note in thick, decisive-looking writing: 'Thought you might like to borrow this. E.M.' She stared at the note for a full minute, trying to work out what McNeill's motives were in sending her the book as well as the gloves. Quickly she began to rifle through the book, but gradually her fingers slowed as the illustrations held her eyes. Here were flowers in abundance, all delicately painted as if the artist had found it a labour of love, taking endless pains to portray each flower, bud and leaf as closely to its original colours as possible. It wasn't a new book, the pages were well thumbed and the jacket worn at the edges, as if it had often been stuffed into a pocket and taken along for reference on a walk over the hills.

If it had been new Marnie would have had no hesitation in sending it back, guessing that he had only used the phrase 'to borrow' as an excuse to make her a gift in repayment for helping Brutus. But there could be no doubt that this was a genuine loan; it was obviously a well-loved book and one he would want back. She began to read, fascinated by the descriptions of the flowers, many of which were entirely new to her, and entranced by the Hebridean names for them. Yes, here was the primrose, with the name morning star in brackets beside it. She could hardly wait for the other flowers to come out so that she could go and look for them.

Marnie left her finger in the place, let her gaze settle on the gloves for a long moment, and then turned her head to look out of the window to McNeill's house. She realised that he had been very clever, guessing her love for wild flowers and pandering to it, and merely

replacing the gloves, but being careful not to send anything that she would instantly reject. So why had he
done it, and did she keep them or not? To be in a
position where she would have to be grateful to him
would be intolerable, of course, but this ... Marnie
bit her lip, wondering what to do. Did she really want
to be on borrowing book terms with the McNeill man?
Or on any terms at all for that matter? She looked
rather longingly at the book. Ever since she could remember she had loved flowers, especially wild ones,
and as a child had come home with great bunches of
them so that the vases in the house were always full, so
many that her stepmother had had to find her empty
jam-jars and bowls to take them all.

Her mind went back to a picnic when they had all
been together, playing cricket afterwards with her
father at the wicket and her stepmother bowling, and
they had all shouted and laughed at her because she
kept wandering off to pick daisies. And Sue had come
running after her and said ... Her thoughts came to a
sudden abrupt stop. Sue would never laugh again,
never see the daisies growing in the grass. Hastily she
bundled the book back into its wrapping and without
giving herself time to think ran out into the night,
stumbling on the uneven road, the air cold through
her sweater. What right had she to look at flowers when
Sue never would again? She fumbled with the latch of
McNeill's gate and swung it noisily back on its hinges.
Inside the house Brutus began to bark. Marnie ran
down the path and groped for the letter box. She'd
just found it when the door was pulled open and
McNeill stood on the threshold, looking at her in some
astonishment. Marnie blinked in the sudden light and
thrust the book at him.

'I don't want this, do you hear me? I don't want it!'
she shouted at him wildly.

He just stood there, making no move to take the
book from her, but Marnie gave a little sob and pushed
it into his hands, then she turned and ran blindly back
down the path, bumping into the gate post in her haste,
then on down the road to the haven of the square of
light emanating from her open front door.

It was the next day before Marnie realised that she
hadn't returned the gloves as well as the book, but by
then she had a drugged but restless sleep behind her, a
night in which the nightmare had come again, breaking
through into her subconscious and going on and on,
and she unable to wake because of the sleeping pills
she'd taken to try and prevent such a thing happening.
So she lay huddled in bed, feeling bone weary but
afraid to go back to sleep again, her eyes dark, her
head feeling like lead.

The weather, too, had changed, as only the weather
round the Western Isles can. She could hear it howling
round the house, tearing at the windows, as if it sought
to find its way in, to lay its icy hold on her. Marnie
shivered and pulled the blankets closer around her.
What was the point of getting up? She would only have
to light the fires to keep the place warm; it was easier
and cheaper to just stay in bed. But she wasn't
naturally lazy and presently she got up and dressed by
the warmth of the electric fire. Afterwards she picked
it up to carry it downstairs and remembered that the
generator was getting low on fuel again, she'd have to
fill it up soon. But not today; today she felt as bad as
when she had first come here and she had no impetus
to do anything but sit on the settee and listen to a
concert on the radio.

The next two days were equally bad, both in mood and weather, and Marnie spent them listlessly by the fire, reading or just gazing into space most of the time. The batteries in the radio had given out and she certainly wasn't going out in this weather to buy more. On the third day the rain stopped, thank goodness, but it was still grey and cloudy and very cold, a film of frost everywhere that didn't melt all day. In the afternoon Marnie wrapped herself up and went outside to chop down some more of the shed; her wood supply was very low and she was afraid it wouldn't last all evening. There wasn't a great deal of the shed left now, just the main uprights holding the corrugated iron roof, a framework of thick pieces on which the planks had been nailed, and about a dozen planks along the last wall. Marnie pulled these off without difficulty and chopped them up. The stack didn't look very high; enough perhaps for tonight and tomorrow, but not much more than that. She looked at the shed and decided to chop up the framework as well. She started pulling off the horizontal, waist-high pieces and had got to the last piece when there was a strange, groaning sort of noise and what was left of the shed started to lean drunkenly towards her.

Marnie gaped at it unbelievingly for a minute and then started to move backwards. The structure had moved slowly at first, but then the whole weight went on to the weak corner post which suddenly collapsed so that the roof came hurtling down very fast in a shower of wet rust and moss. Marnie turned to run, but the beam fell askew and caught her a heavy blow on the head. She stumbled and fell directly in the path of the falling roof. For a few seconds she tried to protect herself, putting her arms over her head and trying to drag herself away, but then the sheets of corrugated iron came crashing noisily down on top of her. Marnie felt a sharp, searing pain in her left leg. She tried to put a hand down to reach it, but before she could do so everything seemed to go hazy and she blacked out.

It was very dark when she came round. Rain splashed on to her face and she could hear it rebounding noisily on the sheets of corrugated iron that lay jumbled around her. Her head felt terrible, as if someone was turning a screwdriver in her brain. Nausea rose in her throat and she had to fight it down, taking deep breaths and willing herself not to be sick. After a while it subsided and Marnie tried to move. There was something heavy lying on her legs; she couldn't see it, but it felt like another upright with a sheet of iron still attached to it, and it was impossible to get a grip on it the way she was lying. She tried to turn round, ignoring the ache in her head, but when she tried to move her legs a white-hot pain shot through her left one and she passed out again.

The rain soaked through her jacket and it was very cold. When she opened her eyes for the second time she immediately began to shiver uncontrollably. She just had to get out of here or she'd freeze to death. She tried to shout for help, but gave it up after a few minutes. Who was there to hear? She was on her own. Grimly she reached down to the debris that pinned her legs. It was lying at an angle, balanced on something else to the right of her. If she could just manage to lift or prop it up she might be able to wriggle out. Scrabbling around with her hands, Marnie found some pieces of planking and used one as a lever to try and lift the iron sheet. Sweat broke out on her forehead as she exerted all her strength. Was it lifting? Was it?

Yes, the sheet had definitely begun to move. There was a sharp snapping sound as loud as a shot, and the piece of planking broke in two.

'Oh no!' Marnie sank back in despair and lay there for several minutes, recovering her breath and with tears running down her cheeks. But she wouldn't give up so easily, she *wouldn't*. Her groping fingers found another piece of wood right at the end of her reach, a thicker piece from the framework this time. She pulled at it with her fingertips and it slowly came nearer by a fraction of an inch at a time. Then she tried again and eventually managed to drag it towards her. She felt along it excitedly. It was really too long to use as a lever, but it would have to do. Inserting it under the corrugated iron she again exerted all her strength to lift it off.

Her head felt as if it was bursting and her arms as if they were going to break, but at last the sheet lifted half an inch, then an inch. Marnie kicked with her heels while still trying to retain her grip of the bar. She wriggled backwards and then dragged her legs clear just as her strength gave out and the sheet clanged down to the ground.

For a while Marnie remained on her knees, just recovering her strength, her breath coming in deep, ragged pants. She tried to stand up, but everything started to swim round her again, so she crawled on hands and knees to the back door, pushing it open and collapsing on to the kitchen floor in infinite gratitude.

Shivering violently with cold, her teeth chattering uncontrollably, she pulled herself up by the electric cooker and turned it on, the hotplates, oven, everything. God, she was so cold, so terribly cold. Scarcely able to control her own movements, she managed to unzip her sodden anorak and take it off, letting it fall to the floor. For a few minutes she held her hands over the hotplate until some feeling returned and her hands began to tingle. Then she turned her attention to her leg. Her jeans were sliced through on the outside of her left leg, a few inches above the knee, and there was a steadily growing bloodstain all around the cut. Dizziness and nausea threatened to overcome her again as she looked at it and she had to cling on to the edge of the sink to stop herself falling. The pain in her head sharpened as she swayed and furry black dots swam in front of her eyes.

Fiercely she told herself that the wound had to be dressed, she couldn't just leave it like that. Vaguely she remembered that she'd seen a first aid box somewhere and forced her mind to think. Now, where was it? In the kitchen or the bathroom? The room began to swim again and she gripped the sink hard. Think, damn you, think! Where had she seen it? Her eyes ran round the kitchen and then she remembered. Yes, that was it; in the top of the cupboard. She managed to cross the kitchen and take the box down, letting it fall on the table with a clatter. It contained everything she needed: bandages, lint, antiseptic cream, Dettol, cottonwool.

The kitchen had warmed up considerably now and Marnie wasn't shivering quite so badly. She filled a bowl with water without too much difficulty and then gingerly began to take off her jeans. Pain shot through her leg as she tried to ease the material away from the wound and she had to sit down hurriedly on a chair and wait a few minutes before she could go on. But when she'd laid it bare, she was thankful to see that the cut didn't look too bad; it was long, about four inches and jagged, but she didn't think it went too deep and would need stitches. She cleaned it up as best she could and applied a dressing, using up a couple of bandages to hold it in place.

Filling up a kettle, she put it on to heat, while she pulled herself awkwardly up the stairs to her room. The room was freezing cold, but even so it was a relief to take off her wet things and towel herself dry. She would have liked to have just lain in a hot bath to soak, but with the dressing on her leg that was impossible, and besides, the water would take too long to heat up. The plumbing and water heating arrangements in Taornish Cottage left much to be desired. Marnie put on her thickest nightdress with a woollen sweater over it, a pair of bedsocks, and pulled the eiderdown off the bed and hobbled downstairs with it. The electric fire was on in the sitting-room, had been ever since she'd gone out to the shed to chop the wood, and it wasn't too cold in there. The open fire had died right down, but she managed to poke some life into it and put on the few remaining pieces of wood that were stacked in the hearth. With the water from the kettle she made herself a hot orange drink, putting in plenty of sugar, and used the remainder to fill two of the hot water bottles. She would have to boil another kettle for the other two. Tiredly she turned off the cooker, then carried her drink back into the sitting-room where she wrapped herself in the eiderdown and half-lay on the settee in front of the two fires while she drank it.

Gradually warmth began to come back into her body, but her head still ached abominably and she felt very tired. Her watch had stopped and she hadn't thought to look at the clock in the kitchen, but it was very dark and the wind and rain still raged outside.

Marnie huddled deeper into the eiderdown after she'd finished her drink, thinking that she would just wait until the wood fire died down again before she went up to bed. She was still so cold and so tired. But her eyes began to close and soon she was asleep.

She slept for a long time and when she woke faint daylight filtered into the room through the gaps in the curtains. It was cold in the room again, the fire had gone out and the electric fire, too, wasn't working. Vaguely Marnie realised that she had forgotten to put more fuel in the generator. She ought to go and do it now. But she was warm in the eiderdown and her head felt terrible. Her leg, too, was hurting and she felt just too ill to move. For the rest of that day she lay on the settee, dozing fitfully or lying huddled under the eiderdown, but as night fell again she began to feel terribly hot instead of cold. Feverishly she pushed the cover aside. Stabbing pains as fierce as red-hot needles shot through her bad leg and her body was covered in sweat. She longed for a drink of cold water, but when she tried to stand her legs gave way beneath her and she fell back on to the settee. All night she lay there again, sometimes burning hot, sometimes shivering violently with cold.

It was some time before the banging on the front door penetrated to her brain. At first she thought it was only a repetition of the painful thudding in her head, but when she at last realised that someone was there and calling her name she tried to call out, but her throat was too dry and sore and she could only manage a feeble croak.

The banging came again, louder. 'Marnie? Marnie, are you in there?' Even through the thickness of the panelling she recognised McNeill's voice.

Turning red-rimmed eyes towards the door, Marnie again tried to shout, but the effort hurt her and she began to cough. The banging stopped and there was silence. Two large tears ran down her pale cheeks. He'd gone. He must have thought that she was deliberately ignoring him again and had gone away in disgust. With a sob she tried to sit up and go after him, but everything went round and she fell forward on to the floor. Oh, God, she felt so ill and so weak, so terribly weak, she just didn't have the strength to help herself. She lay on the floor and cried in utter despair, beating her fists uselessly against the carpet.

She didn't hear the back door open or McNeill walk in. She was only aware that he was there when he exclaimed, 'What the hell——?' and knelt down beside her.

Marnie stared up at him unbelievingly. 'I—I thought you'd gone,' she gasped on a sobbing croak.

He put his hand on her forehead. It felt infinitely cool. 'You're burning up. What the hell happened?'

She tried to tell him, but began to cough again.

'Never mind. You can tell me some other time.' He pulled the eiderdown off the settee and wrapped it round her, then put an arm under her back and the other under her legs to lift her up. His grip tightened and Marnie let out a rasping scream of pain as his fingers pressed on to her cut leg.

Immediately he let go. 'Marnie, what is it?' he demanded urgently.

'My—my leg. I cut it.' She lay on the floor, biting her lip against the pain.

McNeill swore and unwrapped the eiderdown. She felt him lift up the skirt of her nightdress and then he swore again, in Gaelic. The irrelevant thought came to her that people always swore in their native tongue, and she said mumblingly, 'You must be an islander if you swear in Gaelic.'

McNeill's hand pulled her nightdress down again and then she felt his fingers gently smoothing the hair from her face. 'Of course I am, *mo ghraidh*, did you doubt it?'

He covered her again and lifted her very gently into his arms. Marnie lay there quietly, feeling strangely safe and secure, quite sure that he would take care of her. She felt the cold air of morning on her face as he carried her out into the open and along the road and she snuggled her head deeper into his shoulder. There was nothing to worry about, the McNeill man would take care of her. She began to drop back into semi-consciousness and was only vaguely aware of being carried up some stairs in another house and laid in a big double bed. He made her sit up while he took off her sweater and there was a strangely grim look on his face when he realised how wet with perspiration it was. Her bedsocks must have come off when she was thrashing around in a fever, and now he tucked her bare feet into the bed and pulled a big, soft duvet over her.

He felt her forehead again and then went to leave the room. Marnie pushed the duvet aside in a panic and tried to sit up.

'McNeill! Don't leave me. Please. Please, don't leave me.'

Immediately he turned and came back to sit on the edge of the bed. He took hold of her hand and Marnie gripped his tightly, fiercely, as if her feeble strength was enough to make him stay. With his free hand he gently pushed her back on the pillows.

'I'm only going downstairs to use the phone. I have to send for a doctor. I won't be gone more than five minutes.'

Marnie stared at him with fever-racked eyes. 'P-promise.'

'Promise.'

Slowly, reluctantly, she let go of his hand.

He smiled at her, his eyes warm. 'That's my girl!' His fingers tightened for a moment on her shoulder, then he stood up abruptly and hurried from the room.

Whether he kept his promise or not, Marnie never knew. She relapsed into a fevered state and was hardly conscious of someone stripping off her damp nightdress, of sponging and drying her unbearably hot skin and then helping her into a warm, clean nightgown. Or of someone touching her head gently, finding the lump on it, and then doing something with her leg that made her cry out in pain. For a few seconds then she came to the surface and saw a strange man bending over her and beside him a woman that looked vaguely familiar. But he wasn't there. He'd said he'd stay and he wasn't there.

'McNeill.' She called his name and the woman tried to soothe her, told her to be quiet, but Marnie pushed the woman away and again called his name. And suddenly he was there, holding her hand again, talking to her, but the other man did something to her leg, something that hurt sharply like the sting of a wasp, and she slowly slipped into unconsciousness.

CHAPTER FIVE

IT was three days before Marnie became fully aware of her surroundings, vaguely she remembered people being there, doing things to her, or just sitting in the chair beside the bed, but they had only been shapes, unreal and insubstantial. Not like the people in her tossing, delirious dreams. They were all too real—Sue and Alan, her father. She cried out to them feverishly, moaning and tossing on the pillows, but always someone had been there to calm her, to give her a drink of water and wipe her face with a cool flannel until her sleep had become peaceful again.

Now when Marnie opened her eyes she recognised the woman sitting quietly knitting in the chair. It was Morag Ferguson. Marnie studied her for a moment and then looked round the room. It was quite large and very bright and airy, with a range of elegant, white-painted fitted wardrobes along one wall, light-coloured wallpaper and several pictures on the walls. The duvet cover that lay over her was navy and white checked and in the full-length mirror over in the corner she could see that there was a shag-pile navy blue carpet on the floor. It was a very tastefully decorated room but very unfeminine, no dressing-table or soft colours. Marnie stared round the room and wondered where on earth she was and how she'd got there.

She turned her head towards Mrs Ferguson again and saw that the elder woman had stopped knitting and was looking at her with a warm smile on her face.

'Well, now, *mo ghaoil*, so you're awake at last. And
there we were all thinking that you were going to be
like the princess in the fairy tale and sleep for a
hundred years!'

Marnie smiled at her weakly. 'Have I been asleep
for so long?'

'Thrue whole days and nights.' She put a lined hand
on Marnie's forehead. 'Och, you're a lot cooler now. Is
there anything I can get you, lassie?'

'No, I'm fine, thank you.' Her brows drew together.
'Please, is this your house?'

Mrs Ferguson looked disapproving. 'No, it is not.
'Tis Ewan McNeill's house you're in—and in his very
own bed. Though why he could not have carried you
the few yards more to my house, I dinna ken. And
here's Dr Mackay saying that you're on no account
to be moved yet awhile, so I canna take you to my
house where Katie and I could look after you
properly.'

Marnie looked at her rather dazedly, hardly able to
take it all in. But it seemed that she was in the McNeill
man's house, and in his bedroom. Yes, it looked like
his type of room; the colours bold and hard with no
hint of softness anywhere. But why had he brought
her here and not just phoned for an ambulance and
had her taken to the nearest hospital? And Mrs
Ferguson must have thought the same, for she obviously disapproved of her being here. The memory of
someone undressing her, of bathing her, suddenly
came back and Marnie felt herself flush hotly; had
those cool, capable hands belonged to the McNeill
man? Had they?

'Why, lassie, you've gone all red. Are you feeling
badly?' Morag asked, concern in her face. 'Wait now

while I go and get you a cool drink.'

She bustled out before Marnie could speak and came back with a tall glass of blackcurrant drink.

'The doctor will be by before long,' Morag told Marnie while she drank it. 'He usually comes just before midday.'

Marnie leaned back against the headboard, wondering how she could tactfully ask if it had been McNeill who had handled her so intimately, but even as she was trying to find the words tiredness overcame her again and she fell asleep almost immediately.

When the doctor, a keen-eyed man in his early forties, arrived, Marnie woke again, and was told that her leg was mending well and hadn't needed any stitches.

'In time you won't even have a scar,' he told her reassuringly. As if that mattered. He took her pulse and asked, 'Had you been ill lately? Before you came to Culla?'

Marnie's wrist moved under his fingers and he shot her a quick glance. 'I was in hospital for a few weeks,' she admitted reluctantly.

'What was the matter?'

She shook her head. 'Nothing, really. I—I was in a car accident and it—it affected my nerves.' Her voice tailed off and she looked away.

'I see. Well, that probably explains why your resistance was so low. You've had a bad chill, a very bad one. For a while we were afraid it was going to develop into pneumonia. But you've been lucky; you're on the mend now and another week in bed should see you completely recovered.'

'A week?' Marnie stared at him in horror. 'But I can't stay here for a whole week!'

'Oh, yes, you will, young lady. And you'll take things easy for another month after that. You're as weak as a kitten, and if you try to do too much too soon you'll make yourself really ill.'

He spoke forcefully, and it somehow seemed incongruous in his rich Scots accent, but there was a stern warning in his voice that Marnie couldn't ignore. Tiredly she nodded and he went away, satisfied that she would obey him.

She didn't see McNeill until later that evening. Morag had brought her up a beautifully cooked meal and had afterwards helped her to wash herself and brush her hair. When she'd gone Marnie lay back on the pillows and realised just how right the doctor had been; she was so weak that even washing had exhausted her. She heard the front door bang shut below her and Morag's footsteps going down the path. So now she was alone with the McNeill man.

His knock came about half an hour later. Marnie pulled the duvet closer around her and said rather hollowly, 'Come in.'

'Hallo, how do you feel?' He came in and closed the door.

'Much better, thank you.'

'Good.' He walked round to the other side of the big bed and hooked forward a chair. He was wearing light tan cords and a striped shirt under a V-necked sweater of a matching but darker shade of tan. It came to her suddenly that he was very attractive; not handsome exactly, his features were too hard for that, but there was something about him that would attract women like a magnet. Women who were interested in men, that is. Personally she'd never trust another man again.

He sat down, but before he could speak, Marnie said stiffly, 'I'm afraid I've put you to a great deal of inconvenience.'

'Not at all,' McNeill returned smoothly. 'That's what neighbours are for.'

Looking down at the duvet, she went on, 'It would have been better if I'd gone into hospital.'

'Very likely,' he agreed laconically. 'But as there isn't any hospital on Culla, it would have been a little difficult.'

At that she turned to look at him. 'No hospital? But what do people do when they're very ill or injured?'

'Then we have to radio to Skye and ask them to send over a Loganair ambulance plane to the airstrip near Ardsay.'

'So why . . .'

'It was blowing a gale at the time, if you remember. We would have had to wait for the weather to change, but in any case Dr Mackay said that you'd be all right here so long as he kept a close eye on you.'

'I see.' She lowered her head again so that her face was hidden by the curtains of her hair. 'I'm sorry to have caused you so much trouble. And—and I want to thank you for—for bringing me here, of course.'

McNeill regarded her bent head thoughtfully for a minute and then laughed. 'Of course,' he repeated mockingly, then added harshly, 'You're a poor liar, Marnie. Having to thank me makes you want to choke. Gratitude is the last thing you want to feel towards anyone.'

'That isn't true,' Marnie protested. 'I—I am grateful to you, for taking me in, and giving up your bed.'

An amused look came into his grey eyes. 'Do you think I'm sleeping on the floor or something? I assure you I'm not. I dumped you into this bed because the one in the guest room wasn't made up at the time.'

'I see.' Somehow the word 'dumped' jarred. It was as if he looked on her as nothing more than a sack of potatoes. 'All the same, now that I'm better I must insist on giving you back your bed.'

'There's really no point; I've taken my gear into the other room. You might as well stay here now.'

'That isn't quite what I meant,' Marnie told him. 'I meant that tomorrow I'll be going back to my own cottage; I won't have to—to trespass on your hospitality any longer.'

McNeill crossed his legs and leant back against the chair, putting his hands behind his head. His top lip curled a little as he regarded her. 'Trespass on my hospitality,' he aped mockingly. 'I wonder if you know how utterly ridiculous that sounds.' He didn't move at all, but suddenly his face and voice became menacing. 'Doc Mackay said that you're to stay in bed for another week and that's where you're going to stay, even if I have to tie you to the bed.'

Marnie glared at him. 'That will *not* be necessary. I merely wanted to relieve you of the extra trouble I must be causing you.'

'Liar!' McNeill said contemptuously. 'You just want to go on with your big martyr act and go back to a masochistic existence where you can have a lovely time feeling sorry for yourself.'

Eyes wide in her ashen face, Marnie stared at him

appalled. 'That—that isn't true!'

'No?' he asked tauntingly. 'Then why want to go back?'

She turned her head away and bit her lip to stop the tears forming in her eyes. 'You wouldn't understand.'

'You said that once before,' he pointed out wryly. 'But it hasn't changed my opinion.'

'You—you pig!' Marnie burst out. 'How can you treat me like this?'

He lowered his arms and leaned forward. 'What's the matter, Marnie? Are you used to having your men treat you like a piece of fragile porcelain, ready to do anything to please you? You don't like it when people see through you, when they're not bowled over by your looks, do you?' He stood up and towered over her. 'Well, the way I see it you're just a miserable little coward who thinks the world has come to an end because for once things haven't gone your way. And until the time comes when you start acting like a grown woman, then that's the way I'm going to treat you.' He looked down at her contemptuously. 'And don't think I'm going to let you go back to your cottage until you're completely well; I don't want the death of even someone as cowardly as you on *my* conscience.'

For a few seconds longer he glared down at her, but when she didn't look up or speak, he turned on his heel and walked out of the room.

Marnie lay with her head buried in the pillows, gripping them tightly. How dared that pig of a man say such cruel things to her! It wasn't fair. And they certainly weren't true! But as she lay there in the quietness of the room, she came to realise that perhaps coming to Culla had been a form of self-punishment and not the seeking for peace and privacy that she'd told herself it would be. She'd known that the conditions would be harsh, the weather cold and the winds fierce, the days short and the nights terribly long. But still she had come, although she could easily have found the privacy she sought in more hospitable climates.

Was that what her soul craved; to be punished for what she'd done? For a means of expiating her sister's death through her own suffering? She tried to concentrate, asking herself whether bringing the shed down on top of her had been a deliberate act of her subconscious. She'd known that the upright was insecure because McNeill had already told her so, but still she had gone on pulling the framework down until the post had been unable to stand the strain. Marnie bit her lip. Did that mean that subconsciously she wanted to die? But if so, why didn't she just walk into the sea or off the edge of the cliffs? Or would that be too simple? Why make it look like an accident? To save her parents further grief? Marnie stirred restlessly. It was all too difficult, too complicated, and her head had begun to ache. But one thing was for sure: McNeill had said that he didn't want to have her death on his conscience, but he didn't know the half of the hell she was going through with her sister's death on hers. She heard a noise by the door and looked up quickly. McNeill hadn't shut it properly and Brutus was pushing it open. He came and sat down near the bed, and he was so big that he could rest his head on the covers. Marnie smiled and reached out to gently stroke him and he licked her wetly in response. Still stroking his head, she let her thoughts drift away from her own troubles and soon she was asleep.

When Marnie awoke it was morning. The dog had gone and someone had come in to turn off the light, for the room was in that semi-darkness where only the curtains shut out the daylight. Somewhere downstairs she could hear voices and then a girl's laugh rang out, clear and happy. Marnie pulled herself up in bed and wondered what the time was, surprised that she'd slept for so long, and without sleeping pills. They, of course, were back in her own cottage, and she wondered uneasily if anyone had found them. The thought of the cold cottage dispirited her; she would have to go back there soon, but the thought of it certainly didn't fill her with enthusiasm.

As she sat up there was the sound of light footsteps running up the stairs, a quick rap on the door, and then it opened as a girl about her own age put her head round the door.

'Och, you're awake. Good.' She came into the room and moved to open the curtains to let in shafts of spring sunshine, and Marnie saw that she had soft brown curly hair, pleasant features, and a lovely warm smile that lit up her whole face.

'I'm Katie Ferguson,' the girl told her as she came to stand beside the bed. 'My mother's busy this morning, so I've come along to see to you.' She had a pleasant, lilting accent, but it was nowhere near as broad as Morag's.

'Thank you. But if you could just tell me where the bathroom is, I'm sure I'll be able to manage by myself.'

Marnie pushed the duvet aside and swung her legs out of bed. She stood up, her bare toes sinking into the deep pile of the carpet, and went to take a step, but suddenly everything started to sway around her and Katie Ferguson had to grab her to stop her from pitching forward.

'Oh!' Marnie clung tightly to the other girl's arm. 'I'm—I'm sorry, I feel rather dizzy.'

Katie laughed. 'I'm not surprised—you haven't been on your feet for four days. Here, sit you down again while I get you your slippers and dressing-gown, then I'll help you along to the bathroom.'

The next half hour proved to Marnie just how weak she was; just walking to the bathroom and back exhausted her and she was glad enough to sit in an armchair while she watched Katie change the bed-linen.

Feeling that she had to say something, Marnie remarked stiltedly, 'It's really very kind of you to give up your time to help me.'

'Och, it's nothing. I came before in the evenings, but you were too ill to know who was here. Usually I canna come during the day because I'm off to my work, but as it's Saturday I came over so that my mother could do her baking.'

'Oh, I see.' Marnie had had no idea what day it was; the days had all seemed to merge since she'd been on Culla. 'Where—where do you work?'

'In Ardsay,' Katie replied cheerfully as she shook up a pillow. 'In the bank. The same one as Hector.'

'Hector?'

'My fiancé.' She said it with great pride and couldn't resist looking down at the diamond that sparkled on her finger.

'Oh, yes, I remember. McNeill told me.' Marnie flushed and added with difficulty, 'I'm sorry I didn't come to your—your engagement party, but I . . .'

'Och, think nothing of it,' Katie came to her rescue. 'I ken fine you wouldn'a want to come, but my mother said that you wasn'a to be left out when the whole of Taornish was coming.'

A little silence fell between them and to break it Marnie asked, 'Was it a good party?'

Katie laughed. 'Och, I'll say. There were the half of the menfolk as drunk as lords by the time they went home.'

Marnie smiled a little. 'Yes, I heard them singing.' She hesitated, but couldn't resist asking, 'And was McNeill drunk too?'

'Ewan?' Katie's brows rose in astonishment. 'Och, no, he has a head like rock, that one. He's always the last one standing at any party and has to carry the others home and put them in their beds.'

'He seems to be rather good at that sort of thing,' Marnie remarked wryly.

For a moment Katie didn't get it, then she laughed. 'But it's usually the men he helps home; you're the first girl he's ever had to do it for. Here, your bed's ready again now. Will I help you off with your slippers?'

After she'd helped Marnie back into bed, Katie brought her up some breakfast and went down to talk to McNeill while she ate it. Marnie could hear their voices, Katie's light and carrying, McNeill's deeper and quieter, and their shared laughter. They seemed to be on very good terms, as if they'd known each other for a long time. When she'd finished Katie came up with some books and magazines and took the tray away again. Ten minutes later Marnie heard the front door shut and waited for McNeill to come up to her.

She wondered what kind of mood he would be in; belligerent as usual, she supposed. She'd never had a conversation with him yet without it developing into an argument. That this was largely her own fault she was ready to admit, but he was so damn sure of himself and that he was right, that it immediately put her back up. She pondered on whether it was only with her that he made the sparks fly, or whether he rode roughshod over everyone he disagreed with. The latter probably, she thought sneeringly, unless they were people like Katie and her mother who obviously let him dominate them. Fleetingly, she thought of Katie's Hector, wondering what he'd got that McNeill hadn't, for Katie to prefer him. You'd have thought that if she was on such good terms with McNeill, she'd have chosen him— after all, he seemed to be quite a good catch, if this house and the boat were anything to go by. Certainly no expense had been spared on the house; everything she'd seen was of very good quality and must have cost a bomb to ship over from the mainland. He was good-looking, and he was certainly very masculine. He would make quite a good husband, in fact, if you were the type who didn't mind never being allowed to have an original thought of your own. And sexually? Marnie's skin prickled as she suddenly wondered what it would be like to have sex with McNeill, to have his strong, muscular body in the bed beside her.

Hastily she wrenched her thoughts away, a flush of colour on her cheeks. It was nothing to her what the man was like as a husband, either in or out of bed, and obviously Katie had seen through him too, for she'd chosen someone else. After all, it wouldn't be every woman's idea of happiness to be married to someone who went around as if he was the King of Culla. King of Culla—Marnie repeated the phrase in her mind, liking the sound of it, then rather petulantly reached out for a magazine, wondering how much longer he would be before he came up to her.

But he didn't come all that morning; or if he did Marnie didn't see him, for she fell asleep after an hour or so. She was only aware of him when she felt a light touch on her arm and opened her eyes to see McNeill looking down at her. Hastily she sat up and pushed the hair out of her eyes.

'I'm just about to make lunch,' he informed her. 'Can you manage a steak?'

'Thanks, but I'm not very hungry.' Marnie looked round for her dressing-gown, but it had slipped on to the floor. She reached for it, but he stooped and picked it up first.

'Here.' He casually draped it over her shoulders and Marnie pulled it closer around her. He looked at her frowningly. 'You're not going to start refusing things again, are you? Because if so . . .'

'No,' Marnie said hastily. Her eyes met his and she quickly looked away. 'No, I'm really not very hungry, Katie gave me a big breakfast.'

'Nevertheless you need to eat. I'll cook you an omelette. Do you like mushrooms?'

'Yes. Thank you.'

'Good. It'll take about fifteen minutes.'

He was back in less than that time carrying a tray set with everything she needed. He hadn't forgotten a thing. But he didn't stay, merely gave her the tray and went away again.

Marnie began to feel more than a little piqued. Okay, so it was a mutually accepted thing that they didn't like each other, but that was no reason for him to ignore her, was it? After all, he'd brought her here, she hadn't asked to come, and she *was* a guest in his house, even if an unwanted and unwilling one. Perhaps he was one of those men who couldn't stand being near a sick person at any price, but in that case you'd have thought he'd have taken her to Morag's house in the first place instead of to his own. And what on earth was he *doing* all day? She'd hardly heard a sound all morning.

After half an hour he came to take the tray away, said a brief, 'Anything else you want?' and when she shook her head, gave her only a nod and went downstairs again.

There were some kitchen-type sounds and she heard him talking to Brutus, then his footsteps in the hall, the sound of a door closing, and silence again.

Marnie spent some time trying to figure out what he could possibly be doing: reading, perhaps? But surely no one could just sit and read all day long? Unless he was studying for something. But he was too old to be a student, and besides, he didn't look the type who would be a mature student of anything. He would have known what he wanted to be when he was at school and would have learnt everything he needed to know then. After a time she gave it up and switched on the radio that was built into the headboard of the bed, lay listening to a play until the monotonous sound made her doze off yet again.

In the evening Morag came to give her a meal and help her to the bathroom, and, as the previous evening, after she'd gone McNeill came up to see her. He was carrying a small leather-bound case.

'Can you play backgammon?'

Marnie shook her head in surprise. 'No.'

'Then I'll teach you.'

He sat down in the chair and put the case on the bed while Marnie looked at him indignantly. No, would you like to learn? or would you like to play? just an autocratic decision.

If McNeill saw the mulish look on her face he ignored it, merely opening the case to display the inside, which was lined with some soft material which had long thin arrows of different coloured material in rows of six in both the bottom and the lid of the case. He picked up two lots of ivory counters, half white, half black, and began to set them out on some of the arrows.

'The object of the game,' he explained, 'is to move all your counters—yours are the white ones—to your home. That's that section there, nearest you,' he added, pointing it out to her. 'We have two dice each and take it in turn to shake.'

Marnie lifted her head and looked at him unbelievingly. 'And that's all you have to do, just move the counters round the board?'

'At its simplest, yes. It's slightly more complicated than that, but I'll show you as we go along.'

He explained about being able to use the numbers shown on the two dice separately, and about the danger of only leaving a single counter on an arrow, blots he called them, but apart from that there was nothing in the least complicated about it. Kid's stuff, Marnie thought disparagingly. No more interesting than ludo or snakes and ladders, less in fact. They played a round and she sat back, bored and feeling strangely disappointed. She'd somehow expected more of McNeill than that he'd amuse himself with such childish games.

'Right, now you've got the hang of it, we'll play another game.'

Marnie gave an audible sigh but said, 'Oh, all right, if that's what you want.'

McNeill's hand paused in putting out the counters and she looked up to find him regarding her steadily, a slightly sardonic lift to his brow. But their eyes had hardly met before he had looked down at the counters again.

'Okay, you can have first throw.'

With the air of someone humouring a small child, Marnie picked up the shaker and tossed her dice on to the board.

Ten minutes later the game was over and Marnie was staring at her counters, still over the wrong side of the board or on the bar, while McNeill's side was completely empty. He had completely wiped the floor with her. She looked up at him indignantly. 'How could you possibly have got yours off so quickly? You must have thrown more often than I did.'

His mouth tightened a little at the implied insult, but he merely said, 'Not at all. It was just that I used my head while you just moved counters.'

Marnie frowned, hating to be beaten so over-whelmingly, and wondering what there was in it that she'd missed. 'We'll play another game,' she said de-cisively.

They played three more games and Marnie lost them all, but at least she'd begun to see how he was beating her so easily and had been able to move her counters so that his win became a little harder every time. After the third game he began to put the counters back in the holders.

'But I want to play another game,' Marnie told him.

'Tomorrow. You've done enough for tonight, you're beginning to look tired.'

She leant back against the headboard, knowing that he was right, but perversely annoyed that he had pointed it out. 'I'm quite capable of knowing whether I'm tired or not, thanks,' she said snappily.

His left eyebrow rose. 'Of course,' he agreed mockingly, meaning just the opposite.

Marnie glared at him exasperatedly. 'What is it with you, McNeill? Are you a misogynist or something? That's a woman-hater,' she added, her voice heavy with ridicule.

'I'm fully aware of the meaning of the word.' He leant back in the chair, relaxed, his long legs stretched out in front of him, not at all thrown by her question. Slowly he let his eyes travel over her so that Marnie instinctively put up a hand to close the edges of her dressing-gown tighter together. McNeill saw the gesture and his lips drew into a thin smile. 'No, I'm not a woman-hater. On the contrary, I have a very high regard for some women.'

'Some women?' She had the distinct feeling that she was playing with fire, but couldn't resist asking the question.

'Why, yes. There are some, of course, that I find detestable.'

Marnie looked down at the duvet and began to pick at a piece of thread. 'Such as?'

'Such as nosy, spoilt little brats who're afraid to come right out and ask what they want to know,' McNeill retorted, his voice hardening.

'And just what's that supposed to mean?'

'It means that if you want to know what I think of

you, why beat around the bush, why not just ask me?'

Marnie's blue eyes widened indignantly. 'I do *not* want to know what you think of me. I couldn't care less about the opinion of a—a pompous, overbearing pig like you!'

'Don't you?' McNeill stood up and then slowly lowered himself to sit on the bed. He put a hand on the headboard and leant towards her, his eyes dark and menacing. 'Don't you, Marnie?' he repeated. 'But I think you do.' He put his right hand up to her neck and very gently began to trace the outline of her mouth with his thumb.

Shrinking back against the headboard, Marnie put up her hands to try and push his arm away, but it was like trying to move a tree, and somehow touching him made her pulse beat even faster than it was already. Her eyes stared into his, only a few taunting inches away. Unevenly she said, 'Keep away from me, McNeill.'

An amused look came into his eyes. 'But isn't this what you wanted? Why else accuse me of being a woman-hater?' His hand moved down and slipped inside the top of her nightdress as he began to caress her neck, her throat. 'Surely what you really wanted was for me to prove that I wasn't?'

Bending his head, he caught the lobe of her ear between his teeth and bit gently, his lips warm and soft. 'Or was it just that you wanted to test your female powers on me? See whether I'd succumb to your attractions even though I haven't made a pass before— or perhaps *because* I hadn't made a pass at you.'

His lips moved down to her throat, warm, caressing and Marnie quivered, her breath escaping in a little gasp. She tried to speak, to tell him to go to hell, but somehow the words wouldn't come.

'What's the matter, Marnie?' McNeill went on, his voice soft, insinuating. 'Did this man who let you down shatter your confidence where men are concerned? And then I ignored you.' He laughed lightly. 'You poor girl, no wonder you've been acting like a bad-tempered cat!'

Gently he pulled her down so that her head was resting on the pillows. Marnie opened her eyes and found herself gazing up into his, so close above her, his dark and heavy-lidded with desire. She could hear her heart racing in her chest, so loudly that she was sure he could hear it too. Her lips parted a little and she closed her eyes as his mouth moved nearer and she waited for his kiss, her body tingling with expectation, and a curious feeling of triumph at his easy capitulation.

It was several long seconds before Marnie opened her eyes and saw that he had lifted his head away, was sitting up straight. Her eyes froze on his face, seeing there only contemptuous disparagement. The desire had been only an act to fool her and to make her behave like one. And she'd fallen for it so completely, had really thought that he wanted to make love to her, that he'd fallen into her net. Their eyes met again, but this time Marnie's were full of hurt surprise at his rejection.

McNeill stood up. 'For future reference,' he said bitingly, 'I don't take advantage of women who are guests in my house, especially when they've been ill and are in no state to defend themselves. Not,' he added sarcastically, 'that you showed much inclination to resist. Also, I have no intention of letting myself be used by someone who just wants to find out if she's still capable of attracting men. For that you'll have to find someone who doesn't care whether you use him as a guinea-pig. I'm afraid I prefer my women to want me for myself, not because I happen to be the most convenient object in trousers,' he added with scathing sarcasm.

Marnie flinched and bit her lip hard. Her eyes glittered up at him and she gave a small, thin smile. 'Well, at least I know what you really think of me now, don't I?' she said bitterly.

McNeill looked down at her, his face hard and implacable. 'Oh, no, Adams. You'd be surprised at the half of what I think of you!'

CHAPTER SIX

THE rest of Marnie's week in McNeill's house fell into a pattern. Either Morag or Katie would bring her breakfast up and change the bed and would return in the evening to give her another meal. At about one McNeill would appear briefly with her lunch and then go away until the evening when he would come to her room with the backgammon board again. The second time he brought it up, still smarting from the previous evening, she rudely told him to go to hell, but he merely sat in the chair and said, 'That's the kind of welcome I'd expect from an ill-mannered brat of twelve. Do you want to play or not?' And because she was so bored with being alone she had ungraciously agreed.

On the third day the doctor came again, put a new dressing on her leg and said that she could get up for a couple of hours. Marnie spent them seated in a chair by the window, gazing out at the raging cloudscapes that billowed by. From here she could see her house quite clearly, looking lost and deserted, and she felt no desire to hurry back to its cold discomfort.

They played backgammon again that night and Marnie had her first victory, although she knew that even then she'd been lucky, the dice had been with her. And that night, strangely, they managed to hold a conversation without it ending in a fight. McNeill made some remark about Culla and she asked him a couple of questions about the island. He answered knowledgeably and well and Marnie found herself listening to him with interest and attention. She paused with the shaker in her hand, watching him as he described how an absentee landlord in the nineteenth century had forced many of the islanders to emigrate to Canada so that he could knock down their crofts and use the land for sheep grazing. There was anger in McNeill's eyes and he obviously felt very strongly on the subject. She wondered what he was like when his passions were really aroused, and shivered suddenly, remembering the skilful way he had caressed her the other night, even when he'd only been acting. Somehow she thought that if he had really wanted her nothing would have stopped him from taking her; convention, the rules of hospitality, nothing! That if his emotions ever got out of control he'd let nothing stand in the way of what he wanted.

'It's your turn to throw.'

His reminder brought Marnie out of her reverie and she threw the dice. 'You seem to know an awful lot about the island,' she remarked. 'Were you born on Culla? She moved the counters and handed him the shaker, her fingers touching his as she did so.

'Yes, my father was a man of Culla. He fell in love with my mother when she came here for a holiday one summer but unfortunately they only lived here for a few years before my mother's health gave out and they had to move south to England, only coming here in the summer holidays.'

'Oh, so that's why you . . .' Marnie stopped, realising that she was about to make a personal observation.

McNeill raised his eyebrows. 'What were you going to say?'

Marnie flushed slightly. 'Only that your living in England accounted for your not having a Scots accent.

I couldn't understand how you could be a native of Culla and not have one. And yet you speak Gaelic so well.'

'My father always spoke to me in that language; he believed in keeping it alive and not letting it be stamped out as the English seem to want to do.'

'You speak as if they're the enemy, but you're half English yourself,' Marnie pointed out rather tartly.

An amused look came into his grey eyes, but McNeill merely said, 'So I am. But when I'm living in Culla the Scots half tends to come to the fore.'

'You don't live here all the time, then?' Marnie threw a double six and exultantly moved two of her counters halfway round the board.

'No, I'm usually here only during the summer. In the winter I travel about quite a bit.' McNeill threw his dice—a two and a four. 'How about you? Where are you from?'

Marnie's hands tightened into fists as she realised that by asking him such personal questions she had left herself wide open to the same sort of treatment. 'I lived in London,' she replied shortly, and immediately tried to change the subject. 'You know that book on wild flowers you offered to lend me? I think I would like to read it after all.'

'Ah yes, the one you threw back in my face,' he answered urbanely. 'I remember it well. I'll look it out for you.'

He asked her no more questions and Marnie took care not to ask him any, but after that game he packed up the board and wished her goodnight.

The next day she was able to get up for longer during

the day and that evening McNeill suggested that she might like to go downstairs. Marnie agreed eagerly, she was sick to death of staying in one room and longed for a change of scene; added to which she was curious to see the rest of his house.

He walked slightly in front of her down the stairs, ready to catch her if she felt at all dizzy, but apart from gripping the banister rail rather tightly, Marnie felt fine. Her leg was healing nicely and just had an Elastoplast dressing on it now, and except for getting tired very easily she had little to remind her of her chill.

Although McNeill's bedroom had given nothing away about him, his sitting-room told her a great deal. Most of the walls were lined with bookshelves, but there were also lots of paintings, watercolours mostly, several photographs in Art-Nouveau silver frames and lots of interesting ornaments and knick-knacks on tables and shelves. He settled her in a large, softly comfortable settee near the roughly hewn stone chimney breast where a log fire crackled in the grate. The room was beautifully warm and the wind didn't get through the cracks round the windows and doors and blow the curtains like it did in her cottage.

'Would you like a drink?'

'Yes, please. Vodka and lime, if you have it.'

McNeill crossed to a drinks cabinet and opened the doors to display a large selection of bottles, enough to stock a public bar almost. He poured out the drink and handed it to her.

'Thanks.' Marnie leaned back on the settee and sighed. 'Mmm, this is sheer luxury after Taornish Cottage!'

'But luxury wasn't what you came to Culla for, was

it?' McNeill pointed out as he sat down on the settee at the opposite side of the fire, a drink in his hand.

Marnie gazed down at her glass for a moment and then lifted her head to look at McNeill. He was dressed in black tonight: black cords and soft woollen black polo-necked sweater. It somehow emphasised his height and clearly outlined the muscles in his arms and chest. She remembered suddenly that his ancestors had been the fierce, warlike men of Culla who had gone kilted into battle, sword in hand, their Gaelic war-cries on their lips, and she wondered just how much of the warrior blood still flamed in his veins. He had been lighting a cigarette, but now he blew out the smoke and caught her watching him.

'You didn't answer my question,' he reminded her.

'I know. Because I think you only asked it to try and make me angry again.' Marnie tucked her feet up under her and pulled her dressing-gown over her knees. 'Why do you always try to goad me into an argument, McNeill?'

His mouth twisted in amusement. 'With someone as short-tempered as you even the most innocent remark can lead to a scrap.'

'Are you trying to tell me that that wasn't a loaded question, then?'

'That you didn't come to Culla for luxury?' He shrugged. 'If you wanted the comforts of life there are lots of other places where you could have found them. Most people run to the Westward Isles because they feel that they want to get to grips with nature in the raw; do battle with the elements, if you like. They like to feel that man can still survive against nature in the most difficult conditions. Either that or they're just drop-outs, people who're tired of competing in the rat race and want a slower, more self-sufficient way of life for themselves and their children.' His eyes grew cold and he seemed angry. 'But you're neither of those, really. Certainly not a drop-out and you prefer to stay inside when it rains.'

'Oh?' Marnie's face tightened. 'What does that make me, then?'

McNeill drew on his cigarette and looked at her consideringly. 'At first I thought that you had come here to punish someone, to put on the big martyr act to make someone feel guilty.'

'What made you change your mind?' Marnie asked tightly.

'The fact that no one knows you're here. The postman hasn't called at your house all the time you've been on Culla—he remarked on it to me when I first brought you over to my house and told him to bring any letters for you here instead of your cottage. And also the fact that you've been ill for over a week and haven't asked us to get in touch with anyone. No woman who wanted to punish a man would waste a minute in letting him know that she was at death's door. That would really be guaranteed to bring him running to heel.'

'Why a man? Couldn't it be possible to also want to punish a woman?'

He looked at her speculatively for a moment, then shook his head decisively. 'No. At your age and with your looks it has to be a man.'

'I see.' Marnie took a swallow of her drink, the spirit tasting harsh in her throat. 'So just what is your diagnosis, *Dr* McNeill?' she asked with sarcastic emphasis.

He reached for an ashtray and ground out his cigarette, pressing down on it hard. 'Are you sure you really want to know?'

'Oh, *please*. I'm all ears. And you really can't go this far without finishing it, can you?'

'All right.' He paused for a moment and then said deliberately, 'I think you're trying to punish yourself. That somehow you think that what happened to you was your own fault and you ran as far away from your old life as you could get. To a place where life would be always hard and would remind you every day of what you'd done. You asked me what I think, Adams, so I'll tell you. I think you're trying to bury yourself alive.'

Marnie stared at him, her face white. She set her glass down on the coffee table between them with a snap, spilling the liquid. Swinging her legs round, she stood up. 'I've had enough of this, I'm going back upstairs.'

McNeill made no move to get up, just sat looking up at her. 'What's the matter, Marnie? Does facing the truth hurt?'

Anger flashed in her eyes, making them glisten like sapphires. 'For your information, none of the things you've said applies to me. You're wrong on all counts. I came here because I'd been ill. I wanted to find peace and quiet. Well, that's what I came to Culla to find. But all I did find was you, interfering in my life and refusing to take no for an answer.' Her voice rose, close to hysteria. 'Have you never heard of grief, McNeill? Of needing desperately to be alone?' She stopped abruptly, realising that she was getting carried away. She put a trembling hand to her head and said on a sob, 'Oh, God, why the hell did you have to be here?' Then she turned and ran stumblingly from the room and back upstairs to throw herself on her bed.

It was some time before Marnie could control her emotions enough to even start to think coherently, but when she did she realised with a sick feeling that the last conjecture of McNeill's had been too close to the truth for comfort. But what if it was true, she thought drearily? What did it matter to anyone? Alan hated her, her parents couldn't bring themselves to even see her. She might just as well be buried alive because there was nothing left to live for anyway.

She heard McNeill come upstairs, but it seemed like hours later before she at last fell asleep, and then, almost immediately, the nightmare came. More vivid, more terrifying than it had been for a long time. Marnie stirred restlessly, moaning, and pushing the duvet off as if it was trying to smother her. The car was going along and she knew what was going to happen round the next bend. Then suddenly Alan was standing in the road and was holding out his arms to stop her, but she couldn't stop, she kept jamming her foot hard against the brake, but the car was going faster and faster. Beside her Sue began to scream and she cried out, 'No! Alan! Oh, Alan, no!'

Then someone was shaking her vigorously and a voice was shouting at her. 'Marnie! Wake up. D'you hear me? Wake up!'

Dazedly, still terrified, Marnie became aware that McNeill had hold of her shoulders and was shaking her. She stared at him, still trembling with fear. Then realisation that it was only a dream brought relief flooding through her in a great wave and she put her hands up to her eyes and burst into tears.

McNeill sat down on the edge of the bed, put his arms round her and cradled her face against his shoulder. 'It's all right, *mo ghraidh*. It's all over. You're safe now. Nothing can hurt you. Cry it out and let it go.'

The primitive female need for masculine strength and comfort made Marnie cling to him unashamedly, her tears soaking into the thick towelling material of the navy blue robe he was wearing, and it was only after some little time that she became aware of him as an individual again, and that he was holding her and gently stroking her hair.

Raising her head, Marnie put up her hands in a childish gesture to wipe away the tears. McNeill took his arms away and she sat up. 'I'm sorry,' she said stiffly. 'I'm—I'm afraid I had a rather bad nightmare.'

'One that you get often?'

She nodded, not attempting to deny it. 'It does seem to come back rather a lot, yes.'

He rose and crossed to a chest of drawers, opened the top one and took out a handkerchief which he tossed to her. It was only then that Marnie realised that he wore only pyjama trousers under the bathrobe.

After using the handkerchief to wipe her face and blow her nose, she looked down at it and said unevenly, 'I'm sorry, I obviously woke you up. Is it very late?'

'About two. How long have you been having these nightmares, Marnie?'

'Oh, ages,' she answered, trying to keep her voice light. 'I really ought to be used to them by now.'

'Did you tell Dr Mackay about them?'

She took her head. 'I—I have some sleeping pills to take, but they're over at the cottage.'

McNeill regarded her frowningly for a moment, then said abruptly, 'Do you want to take some now? I'll ge over and get them for you if you'll tell me where they are.'

'No, it's all right.' Head averted, she said slowly, 'I think I'll go back home tomorrow, McNeill.'

Sitting down on the edge of the bed, he put a hand under her chin and lifted her head so that she had to look at him. There was a look on his face Marnie hadn't seen before, half concern, half something that she couldn't fathom. His tone very earnest, he said, 'Look, I know I pushed you too far tonight and I upset you. I'm sorry, it won't happen again. But I can't let you go back to your cottage yet. You must stay here until you're really well enough to be alone.' He waited for her to speak but, when she didn't, added more firmly, 'Don't fight me on this, Marnie.'

Slowly, tiredly, she nodded, knowing that she wouldn't be able to cope alone yet. 'All right, I'll stay.'

'Good.' He stood up and turned to go but Marnie's voice stopped him as he reached the door.

'McNeill. Why did you bring me here?'

He paused and slowly turned to face her. 'If you have to ask that question then you're not nearly ready to hear the answer.' With which enigmatic reply he went out of the room.

He must have told Morag that she'd had a bad night, because they let her sleep late the next morning, and it was almost midday before Marnie woke. Without bothering to ask what she wanted, McNeill brought her up a meal of grilled trout with almonds.

Marnie took the tray from him and sniffed appreciatively, feeling suddenly hungry. 'You're a very good cook,' she commented.

He grinned. 'You forgot to add—for a man. I've had to learn. When you're living alone it's a case of necessity. Stuff out of tins and packets never seems to fill you up.'

Marnie looked at his large frame and could well believe it. He went to leave, but Marnie called him back. 'Would you do something for me, please?'

'Of course. What is it?'

'Would you ask Morag if she'd mind going to my house and bringing me some clothes? And my bag? I don't know what happened to the door key. Do you have it?'

His brows drew into a frown. 'You're not getting any more ideas about going back there, are you?'

'No.' Marnie shook her head. 'I just feel that I'm well enough to get dressed during the day, that's all. It seems to make me feel more like an invalid if I wear nightclothes all the time.'

'Okay, I'll give her a ring and tell her. And don't worry about the key, the door won't have been locked, no one ever locks their doors on Culla. There aren't any thieves and it's easier for the neighbours to come to your aid if you have an accident,' he added with pointed irony.

The clothes were brought for her and it felt good to be properly dressed again. Katie came to keep her company that evening because McNeill was going out, and the two girls sat in the lounge and watched television because there was a serial that Katie was following and didn't want to miss. It was the first time Marnie had watched the television since she'd come to Culla, she'd never bothered to turn on her own, and it seemed weird somehow, as if she'd suddenly become part of the twentieth century again after living for weeks in the past.

Afterwards they talked and the subject inevitably came round to Katie's wedding, which Marnie was surprised to learn was to take place quite shortly.

'Well, there seems no point in waiting,' Katie confided. 'Hector has the flat over the bank for us to live in and it's all furnished. And besides,' she blushed, 'Hector says he doesn'a believe in over-long engagements. If you've made up your mind and you have the means, then what's the point in waiting?'

Marnie smiled at her. 'He sounds a very forceful man.'

'Och, no. He's very kind and gentle. But he said that having made up his mind to take a wife he wanted to be married as soon as maybe.'

A shadow fell across Marnie's face as she remembered her engagement to Alan. She, too, had been keen and eager to get married at first, but her parents had said that she was too young, they must wait until Alan had passed his exams, and somehow the lapse of time had taken the gloss, the first enchantment, if you like, out of their romance. In the end it had become commonplace, almost a habit, like a comfortable old coat she put on whenever she went into the country. For the first time it occurred to Marnie that perhaps Alan had had some justification in turning to her sister. And for going to bed with her? But even now Marnie's mind cringed away from that thought. That had always been one of the hardest things to take.

McNeill got back about eleven and saw Katie home, then came back and sat with Marnie while he drank a nightcap, and told her about the meeting he'd attended in Ardsay. It seemed that a group of speculators were trying to buy up a large piece of land on which to build a very modern, luxury hotel to attract tourists, but the islanders were resisting it for all they were worth in an attempt to keep the island from being overrun by visitors. He spoke eloquently and it was obvious that he felt very deeply on the subject.

'Do you think you'll keep them out?' Marnie asked him.

His jaw thrust forward, strong, determined. 'Oh, yes, we'll keep them out. Even if I have to buy up that land myself.'

Marnie's eyes flew wide in surprise. 'Could you do that?'

He looked up and his eyes met hers. 'If I have to,' he replied evenly. 'But it's not the best way round the problem. It would be better if the land was farmed in small crofts so that the people who work them would have an invested interest in the island and the good of the community. Summer visitors are all right as long as the numbers are reasonable; too many and you get souvenir shops and cafés springing up, the water supply runs out, and the young people start leaving the crofts to make an easier living in the hotels.'

They talked on a while longer, then McNeill rose and said, 'It's almost midnight, you'd better go to bed or you'll feel low again in the morning.'

Marnie took the hand he held out to her and let him help her to her feet. 'I feel much better today. Really.'

'Well enough to go out for a while tomorrow?'

'Out? Where?'

'I want to go and have another look at the piece of land the speculators want to build the hotel on. If it isn't too cold you could come with me. You'll be warm enough in the car if you wrap yourself up. If you're not feeling up to it, then forget it,' he added when he saw her hesitate.

'No, it's not that.' She looked at him uncertainly. 'It's just that I thought perhaps you didn't really want me along, but felt that you couldn't leave me here alone. But I'd be all right by myself. You don't have to—to feel responsible for me.'

He frowned. 'Do you *want* to come tomorrow, or not?'

'Yes, I'd—I'd like to; I haven't seen very much of the island at all.'

'Then that's settled. We'll leave after breakfast.'

Which left Marnie, as she climbed the stairs to her room, still wondering whether McNeill had wanted to take her.

The next day was fine, but there was still a nip of winter in the air and McNeill insisted that she borrowed a sheepskin jacket of his to put over her own thick sweater. He also wrapped a blanket round her legs and turned on the car heater so that she didn't feel at all cold. The tract of land he wanted to see was on the other, eastern coast of the island, and they had to drive through Ardsay to reach it. There were more trees on this side of the island which was sheltered from the worst of the Atlantic winds by the range of hills that separated east from west. The land was flatter too and there were more root crops and fewer sheep.

'You see that old house,' McNeill remarked, pointing at a small stone-built thatched roof building that seemed half sunk in a depression in the ground. 'That's a *tigh dubh*, literally a black house. All the original houses on Culla were built like that, with rounded end walls to withstand the strong winds.'

He pointed other things out to her and told her that once a lot of islanders had had looms in their homes and had spent the winters weaving Harris tweed, but now it was mostly done on power looms in small factories and it had virtually died out as a cottage industry.

'And Morag is one of the few people left who collects the wool from her own sheep and dyes it in the old way, using flowers and lichens she gathers herself on the hills. Then she dyes the wool in a big cauldron and takes it to rinse in the burn.'

'Oh, so *that's* what she was doing,' Marnie exclaimed. 'I saw her when I was out walking on the cliffs once and wondered what on earth she was up to. Does she weave it into tweed?'

'Some of it, but some she knits up into sweaters and things.' His brows drew into a frown. 'That reminds me. I meant to warn you not to go walking along the cliffs, or in the hills for that matter, alone. The mist can come down suddenly so that you completely lose your bearings.'

They came to the area he wanted to see and they drove around while he marked out the boundary on a large-scale map with a red pen. Once they stopped for about ten minutes while he talked to a crofter, but he came back before Marnie could even begin to feel chilly. They were out for only about three hours, but it was enough; Marnie was glad to see the road to Taornish and know that she'd soon be home.

McNeill helped her out of the Land Rover and held the gate open for her.

Marnie paused as she went to go through and pointed to the carved name. 'What does it mean—Seanachaidh?' She struggled with the unfamiliar word.

He smiled. 'It's pronounced Shenna-ka. It means a teller of tales.'

She looked at him questioningly. 'And are you, then, a teller of tales?'

'I'm a writer, yes.'

Her eyes opened wide in surprise. 'You never told me that before.'

Brusquely he said, 'You weren't interested enough to ask me before,' and ushered her up the path to the house.

Morag came over that evening and found Marnie setting the table in the dining room for two places while McNeill cooked the dinner. She asked Marnie how she was and said she looked much better. Marnie assured her that she was and after talking to her for a little longer, Morag went into the kitchen to find McNeill, shutting the door firmly behind her.

After she'd gone, they sat down to dinner, Marnie feeling suddenly and strangely shy being in such a domestic situation with someone she hardly knew. To cover it she asked him about his work and he told her that he wrote both novels and non-fiction. 'I do most of my research during the winter and then come home to Culla to do the actual hard slog of writing.'

'So that's it. I've been wondering what you do all day. The house has always been so quiet while I've been lying upstairs.' She hesitated, then, 'Perhaps you'd lend me one of your books some time? I'd like to read one.'

He glanced at her. 'All right, I'll give you a couple to take home with you. Tomorrow,' he added deliberately.

Marnie quickly raised her head. Trying to keep her voice light, she asked, 'Does that mean you're kicking me out?'

'I'm afraid so. We're starting to offend Morag's sensibilities.'

'Morag's?'

'Yes. The people of Culla are very religious and

rather puritan. Morag always disapproved of my bringing you here, but looks upon it as the duty of everyone to help his neighbour so tolerated the situation while you were so ill. But when she came over tonight and found you up and about it completely altered the situation. She warned me that people would *start talking*, and that you must either go home, or, if you aren't quite well enough yet, go to stay at her house until you are.'

'And do you take orders from Morag?' Marnie asked, laying down her spoon and fork.

McNeill's mouth twisted with amusement. 'Is that a challenge?'

'No, just a question.'

He shrugged slightly. 'In this case, yes. The islanders are great gossips and love any hint of a scandal.'

Marnie flushed and said shortly, 'But there's nothing between us.'

'But they're not to know that, are they? Would you like some brandy?'

'Yes, please.' She frowned. 'It's ridiculous, they couldn't be more wrong.'

McNeill picked up his brandy balloon and swirled the liquid round inside it. He looked at Marnie over the top of it and said calmly, 'Nor could you.'

Marnie looked puzzled and opened her mouth to ask him what he meant, but he quickly changed the subject.

It was almost with a feeling of sadness that Marnie collected her things together the next morning and put on her coat to go back to her cottage. She felt as if she'd lived in the room for ages, it had become so familiar. It was rather like going on holiday and taking possession of a hotel room; it had become part of her life for a while and she had come to look on it as her own, not McNeill's.

He was waiting for her at the foot of the stairs and took the bag with her belongings in it from her.

'Ready?'

She nodded.

'Good. It's quite mild today, luckily.' He opened the front door and Brutus bounded out ahead of them. 'Morag said she'll come round tonight to make sure you're okay.' He raised an eyebrow. 'You won't throw her out this time, will you?'

Marnie smiled. 'No, I won't throw her out. McNeill . . .'

'If you should start to feel ill again don't wait to see if you get better, go straight to Morag or to me. Understand?'

'Yes, of course.' They were almost at her gate. 'McNeill, I wanted to . . .'

'And don't go out for a walk or anything until you're completely better. If you need anything from Ardsay tell Morag and either she or I will get it for you.'

'Yes, all right. Look, McNeill, I . . .'

But they were at her door and he had pushed it open for her.

'Some other time. Go on in. Don't stand around in the cold.'

He pushed her inside and Marnie said, 'But aren't you coming in?'

'No, I've a book to write.'

'But I haven't had a chance to thank you for taking me in.'

But already he was striding back down the path, his hand raised in casual farewell.

Slowly, reluctantly, feeing strangely lonely, Marnie closed the door and stepped into the sitting-room, expecting to find it as she last remembered it: cold, soot-blackened and untidy. But instead it was as she'd first seen it when she'd arrived on Culla, with a log-fire crackling in the grate, clean and welcoming. In the kitchen the store cupboards, fridge and freezer had been replenished and there was a big box full of dry logs for the fire. Her bedroom, too, had been thoroughly cleaned, her clothes laundered, and there was another fire making the room pleasantly warm. Over it all there was an appetising smell of cooking, and Marnie felt no surprise at all when she found a casserole simmering slowly in the oven. She went back to the sitting-room, sat in the chair by the fire, and for the first time since the accident, wept for a reason other than grief.

When Morag came that evening they were both rather reserved, remembering that first time, and Marnie very nearly put her foot in it again when she asked Morag how much she owed her.

The island woman drew herself up and said stiffly, 'I'll no' be asking for payment for helping my neighbours in their time of need.' And she turned to go to the door.

'No, wait, please.' Marnie hurried after her and caught her arm. 'I'm sorry, I didn't mean to offend you. But the freezer has been refilled and there's more food in the cupboards. Someone must have paid for it, and I can't let someone else pay for my food,' she finished on a firmer note.

Morag looked at her for a moment, then nodded in agreement. 'Aye, you canna do that. It was Ewan who paid for it all. He went into Ardsay and brought it all up here himself.'

'I see. Thank you for telling me. And thank you for everything you've done for me, Morag. And I'm sorry I was so—so horrid to you when I first came to Culla. You see, I was very—unhappy at the time and I . . .'

'Och, ist, ist. Hush now. Anyone with half an eye could see that. But now, *feumaidh mi falbh*, I must be going. See that you keep yourself warm now.'

'Yes, I will,' Marnie promised in answer to this and several similar injunctions before Morag finally left.

Marnie sat down by the fire again and looked at her watch. Nine o'clock. McNeill would have finished his meal by now and be doing what? reading, listening to music, watching television. She got up and went into the kitchen, restlessly opening the cupboards and looking at the full shelves. He really had no right to get in all this food without asking her first. She suddenly slammed the doors shut, ran into the sitting-room, put on her coat and wound a scarf round her head, then picked up her bag and a torch and went outside into the pitch darkness of the night.

A light was on in McNeill's sitting-room, she could see thin strips of it at the edge of the windows. She lifted a hand to bang the metal knocker and Brutus immediately began to bark.

McNeill's voice in the hall, a word of command that immediately silenced the dog. Then he said something in Gaelic, '*Co tha'n sud?*' and opened the door. 'Who is it?'

'It's me. I . . .'

'Marnie!' He caught hold of her shoulder and pulled her quickly inside, shutting the door. 'What is it?' McNeill demanded, his voice sharp. 'Do you feel ill again?'

'No, I'm fine. It's just that I . . .'

'Then what the hell are you doing out at night in the cold?'

Marnie looked up at him, surprised by the roughness in his tone. 'I wanted to talk to you.'

He glared at her for a moment, then nodded curtly. 'All right, you'd better come in by the fire.' He led the way into the sitting-room and Brutus lay down in his usual place on the hearthrug, taking up as much room as a small pony. 'Well, what is it?' McNeill demanded.

His abrupt manner making her feel unsure of herself, Marnie said rather awkwardly, 'Morag told me that you'd paid for all the food in my house. I came over to pay you back.'

His face hardened. 'I might have guessed as much. You couldn't even wait until tomorrow, could you? The minute you found someone had done you a favour, you came charging over to pay off the debt. And I suppose you offered Morag money too?'

'Well, yes, but . . .'

'My God, don't you ever learn?' McNeill cut in angrily. 'There are some things you just can't repay with money, and one of them is neighbourliness.'

Stung by his rebuke, Marnie retorted, 'But I certainly don't need charity, from you or anyone. I can afford to pay for my own groceries.'

'All right,' McNeill answered curtly. 'If that's the way you want it, I'll send you the bill when it comes in.'

'Yes, it is the way I want it,' Marnie answered hotly, her anger fanned by his. 'And while you're at it, you can add on the cost of my food and board while I was staying here. There's no way I want to be beholden to you, McNeill.'

'Why, you pigheaded little . . .' He caught hold of her and jerked her towards him, his fingers biting into her arms. 'Someone ought to have put you over his knee and spanked some sense into you years ago!'

'And I suppose you think you're just the man to do it,' Marnie jeered. 'Well, let me tell you some . . .' Her words died in her throat as McNeill's grip tightened and she looked up to see his eyes glinting down at her, a hard, taut look about his face.

'Don't tempt me, lady,' he said unevenly. 'Just don't tempt me.'

He was very close, his face only a few inches above her own. Marnie could see the anger in his face, feel it in the way he held her, but suddenly her own had gone and she could only gaze up at him helplessly, lips parted, eyes wide in her pale face. Slowly, deliberately, McNeill pulled her towards him, his eyes never leaving hers, and then he bent his head as his mouth sought her lips. There was anger still in the way he kissed her, his mouth hard and importuning, taking hers for his own pleasure and not caring whether she was willing or not. His hard lips explored the softness of hers, pushing them apart, forcing her acceptance. And it had been so long since Marnie had been kissed, held, loved. Her body ached, craved for love. She made a little sound under his mouth and moved closer against him, lost in memories.

His lips still taking hers, McNeill released her arm and put up a hand to unwind her scarf so that her hair fell about her shoulders. He caught hold of it, weaving it round his fingers, delighting in its softness. Then suddenly his mouth became more opportuning, more passionate. He pulled her close, holding her hard against him with his other arm. His hand tightened in her hair and he held her head so that she couldn't move, could only stand and let her mouth be ravaged by his. Marnie put her arms around his neck and leant against him, her hips, her thighs moving sensuously.

'Marnie!' His lips left her mouth and began to explore her throat, her neck. She could hear his heart hammering in his chest, feel the pulse in his neck, wild and erratic beneath her fingers.

Slowly Marnie opened her eyes, thinking that Alan had seldom been as uncontrolled as this, never so demanding. Her breath uneven, still lost in desire, she looked up and became aware of McNeill's face above her own, of the naked flame of passion in his dark eyes. As she realised what she'd done, how she had encouraged him, her eyes widened in incredulous horror, and she pushed herself violently away from him.

'You! Oh God, for a moment I thought it was Alan.' She put her hands up to cover her face and didn't see the dark shadow that shut down over McNeill's face.

Taking a few hurried steps away, Marnie turned on him furiously. 'Men! You're all the same. All you ever want is sex! I'm only surprised that you waited till now and didn't try to rape me while I was staying here. You're just as disgusting as all the rest of them, McNeill!' And then she turned and ran stumbling blindly out of his house into the darkness.

CHAPTER SEVEN

Spring seemed to arrive suddenly; for a long time the weather had still been cold with just the hint of warmth in the air, then she woke one morning and found that the wind had gone, the sun was out and the fields were alive with flowers. It was May and the days were much longer, leading up to the almost day long hours of light, and nights that never got completely dark, of high summer. Marnie packed herself a picnic lunch and took to the hills, luxuriating in the feel of the sun on her back and her bare head, enjoying the respite from wind and rain. She lifted her face up to the sun and felt good to be alive. But immediately the happy mood was gone and her step slowed as guilt filled her mind. How *could* she feel this love of life when she had taken her sister's?

The fine weather continued for several days and every day Marnie walked a little further afield as her strength came back. Sometimes Brutus came with her, bounding along at her side and consuming more than his fair share of her sandwiches when she sat down to eat her lunch. Marnie was pleased to have him with her, enjoying throwing sticks and playing silly games with him. He was just what she needed, and gradually the black moods of remembrance and guilt began to go and she would return to her cottage in the evening to cook herself an amateurish meal, then collapse into bed to sleep long and deeply, without the help of sleeping pills and too exhausted to dream.

Of McNeill she saw little; sometimes, if he was going

out or for a walk himself, he would whistle the dog and then Brutus would leap up and leave her side without a second thought, leaving her feeling strangely bereft and lonely. But the weather was so lovely that she would go on walking alone through the grass, her nostrils filled with the scents of purple heather and hundreds of wild flowers.

The mist that McNeill had warned her of came completely unexpectedly. One minute the day was clear and sunny, the next she was surrounded by a thick grey mist, that clung to her clothes and hair in tiny drops of damp moisture. And of course it had to come on a day when she was without Brutus and as she was walking parallel to the cliffs. Marnie tried to walk on, knowing that the path stretched out in front of her, but she couldn't see a thing, and suddenly the noise of the sea pounding on the rocks at the bottom of the sheer cliffs, a hundred feet below, sounded terribly loud in her ears. Hastily she took a couple of steps back and sat down on the ground. Better to sit and wait for the mist to clear than risk a fall.

She sat there for what seemed like hours, gradually getting cold and damp. It was so thick that she couldn't even see her watch properly. She shivered and rubbed her arms, trying to keep warm. She supposed that she ought to have brought a sweater with her, but it had been such a beautiful day when she set out that she hadn't even thought about bringing one. And it was so quiet; the mist seemed to act like a muffler, like a roll of wet grey cottonwool that had wrapped itself round her. Would it *never* clear away? For the first time Marnie began to feel really frightened.

After what seemed an eternity she thought she heard a shout, but it was difficult to tell in the mist; it might only have been the cry of a gull. She strained her ears and gave a gasp of excitement as she heard it again. It had actually sounded like someone calling her name.

'Over here. Hey! Over here!' She yelled at the top of her voice, but the mist seemed to bounce it back at her. She waited, listening, but there was no answering shout and she sat down again dispiritedly, convinced that it must only have been her imagination after all.

Then suddenly a dark shadow loomed out of the mist and Brutus was beside her, licking her face with his big tongue.

'Oh! Stop it. Yes, you're lovely and clever to find me. But stop licking me. I'm wet enough already.'

Marnie pushed the dog aside and realised that McNeill was there too. He put down a hand and hauled her to her feet.

'I might have known that you wouldn't even have a mac with you! Here, put this on.' He slipped a small haversack off his shoulders and pulled out a plastic cagoule, similar to the one he was wearing. Marnie pulled it over her head and found that it covered down to her hips. Immediately she felt warmer. Handing her a silver flask, he ordered, 'Take a pull of this.'

'What is it?'

'Brandy.'

Marnie smiled and laughed a little. 'Shouldn't you have tied it round Brutus' neck?'

McNeill looked at her, then grinned. There were tiny droplets of mist clinging to his eyebrows and to his hair. The relief of having been found had made Marnie forget the circumstances of their last meeting, and now she flushed and concentrated on taking a drink of the fiery liquid, not looking at him as she handed back the flask.

'How did you find me?' she asked, to break the silence.

'I didn't. You owe it all to Brutus. He followed your scent.'

Hearing his name, the dog came over to McNeill and wagged his tail, nearly knocking Marnie over. McNeill grabbed her arm and she regained her balance, but he didn't let go. 'I ought to knock your head off,' he told her roundly. 'I told you not to go walking on the hills alone, especially near the cliffs.'

'I can't be expected to stay in every day just in case a mist comes up,' Marnie pointed out tartly.

'You could keep to the lower ground. What's the matter with you? Have you got a death wish or something?'

Marnie pulled her arm from his grip. 'Certainly not! As soon as the mist came down I sat and waited for it to go away again.'

'You'd probably have had a long wait,' McNeill told her grimly. 'Sometimes it hangs around for days.' He slung the haversack over his shoulder again. 'You ready to start back down?'

'Yes.'

'Okay. Heel, Brutus.' He slipped a short leash on to the dog's collar and said, 'We'd better stick close together because we won't be able to see where we're going. We'll just have to trust the dog to guide us.'

Marnie hesitated, then said reluctantly, 'All right,' and moved to his side, letting him take hold of her arm just above the elbow.

They made slow progress over the uneven, rocky ground; McNeill having the double task of restraining

Brutus from going too fast and holding up Marnie when she stumbled. After about half a mile they stopped to rest and have another swig of the brandy.

'You all right?'

'Yes, just out of breath,' Marnie told him pantingly.

He put his arm round her to support her; it felt as strong and solid as a tree. She leant against his shoulder and he turned to look at her. His arm tightened and she thought that he was going to kiss her again. She stiffened, but he merely put up a hand to wipe the drops of moisture from his hair and looked away again. Which was hardly surprising after her reaction to his first kiss. His *first* kiss? Did that mean she wanted him to kiss her again? Marnie stirred restlessly and straightened up.

'I'm ready to go on now.'

The mist ended suddenly and they were in bright sunshine again, the machair spreading out below them, vivid green and rich with flowers that lay like jewels on emerald velvet. And yet behind them the mist hung like a pall over the hills, completely obscuring them.

Marnie looked back and shuddered. 'Phew, I'm glad to be out of that! Does it happen often?'

'Often enough. In the summer we're always being called out to look for idiot holidaymakers who don't listen to warnings and go out and get caught in it.'

'Idiots like me, you mean?' Marnie said, her voice subdued.

He grinned and then laughed. 'Oh, we make allowances for you; you're a special sort of idiot.'

Marnie glared at him indignantly. 'Well, of all the nerve! I . . .' She broke off abruptly as she realised that she was being teased. For a moment her face was a mixture of emotions, then she grinned ruefully. 'I suppose I deserved that. I'm sorry, I know I'm an awful nuisance to you. You must be cursing me.' She looked at him and smiled, her blue eyes coming alive. 'But next time I get into a scrape just send Brutus.'

It was a moment before McNeill answered, and then his voice sounded strange as he said, 'Maybe I'll do just that.'

They walked on to her cottage and at the gate he turned and said casually, 'I'm taking my boat out to-morrow for a cruise round the island. Do you want to come along?' Then, seeing her hesitate, and correctly guessing the reason, he added shortly, 'No strings.'

Marnie's head came up at that and her eyes met his, and held. After several long seconds she nodded. 'Thanks, I'd like that.'

'Okay, be ready to leave about nine.'

Then he turned and walked on to his own house, Brutus walking at his heels, leaving Marnie looking after him and wondering just why she'd said yes.

But McNeill kept his word and didn't attempt to make another pass at her, treating her as a friend and making her help him with the boat. It was a perfect day; the sun shining warmly, the sea smooth as glass, and Culla looked almost ephemeral, like a fairy island that would disappear with the night, only the cloud of mist that still lay over the hills convincing Marnie of its solidity. At lunchtime McNeill turned the boat and sailed westward for a few miles to a small island that he told her 'was strictly for the birds', and she saw that it was literally true. The whole island was a nature reserve and had been handed over to the seabirds. There were thousands of them swirling about the sky, squawking and screaming, their raucous cries echoing off the cliffs which were covered with their nests.

McNeill pointed the different types out to her: guillemots, puffins, razorbills, stormy petrels, kittiwakes—the list seemed to be endless. He anchored the boat off the cliffs and they sat on deck and ate rolls filled with thick slices of smoked ham as they watched the antics of the birds, squabbling among themselves or diving like folded umbrellas into the sea as they tried to catch any fish that were unwary enough to swim near the surface.

Afterwards McNeill let her take the wheel and showed her how to steer against the wind and how to read the compass. They anchored in Taôrnish bay just as the warmth began to go out of the sun and Marnie walked up from the beach with him, tired and windswept, but feeling strangely content. She'd had a wonderful day, and she told him so, unreservedly.

McNeill nodded, but looked her over critically, a frown between his brows, seemingly unaware of the glow of colour on her cheeks and a brightness in her eyes that had never been there before. 'Don't you ever wear a skirt?' he demanded.

Marnie's eyes flew wide in surprise. 'Why, yes, but I . . .' She stopped and eyed him warily. 'Why should I need to wear a skirt, McNeill?'

'There's a *cèilidh* on Saturday night. At Morag's house. Will you come?'

'A *cèilidh*—that's a sort of party, isn't it?'

'Not as you mean it. It's really just a get-together of friends and neighbours to gossip and perhaps dance a little.'

Marnie shook her head decisively. 'No. I don't feel that I could go to something like that yet.'

'You're afraid?' There was a definite sneer in McNeill's voice.

Marnie's face paled and her nails dug into her palms, Her chin came up defiantly, but then she bit her lip and looked away. 'I—I don't know.'

McNeill put a thumb under her chin and lifted her head. 'I'll be going there at eight. I'll knock for you on the way in case you change your mind.'

She nodded, 'All right.' But her lashes came down over her eyes, hiding her feelings. She stepped away from him, said 'Thanks for today,' and hurried on down the road.

For the rest of the week Marnie was convinced that she wouldn't go to the *cèilidh*, but on Saturday morning she somehow found herself washing her hair and looking out the two dresses she'd brought with her and which were still in the bottom of her suitcase where she'd stuffed them in anyhow when she'd left London. London! Marnie pulled out one of the dresses and looked at it. It was of cream, silky material with a loose straight skirt and a gathered top with just thin shoulder straps. And there was also a loose jacket with three-quarter length sleeves to go over the top. The last time she'd worn it was to a sophisticated cocktail party given by some big company to celebrate the launch of a new product. She remembered she'd been taken there by one of the junior directors and had been introduced to several big names in the commercial and financial world. It had all been very sleek, very rich. And afterwards her escort had taken her out to a nightclub and propositioned her, but she'd flashed her engagement ring at him and that had been the end of that beautiful friendship. There was a pair of shoes to go with the dress, all thin straps and very high heels. She'd break both her ankles before she got halfway down the road to Morag's house wearing those.

Marnie sat and looked at the things for a long time while she tried to make up her mind. Well, it wouldn't do any harm to at least press the dress. And she was still telling herself that it was only to see what she'd look like when eight o'clock came round and found her wearing the dress and shoes, her hair curling softly on her shoulders instead of straight, and with her face pale but beautifully made up. Marnie looked at herself in the dressing-table mirror and began to tremble. This wasn't the Marnie Adams of Taornish Cottage, this was the other one, the one whose fiancé had jilted her, who'd killed her sister.

A knock sounded on the door downstairs, but she didn't go down, just stood and stared, the nervous tension building up inside. 'Marnie?' She heard McNeill open the door and call her name, but still she couldn't move. Then footsteps running up the stairs and his reflection in the mirror as he burst through the door.

One glance and he summed up the situation. 'Oh, good, you're ready. Where's your coat?' Crossing over to her, he swiftly picked up her bag and thrust it into her hands. 'Come on, we don't want to be late.' He took her hand and led her towards the stairs. 'Brutus is waiting downstairs. He loves to go along to a *cèilidh* because he always has such a fuss made of him, but we have to watch him because once he nearly got drunk on some beer that somebody poured into his bowl and now he's got a taste for it.'

He kept on talking while he got her downstairs and helped her into her coat. It was only when he opened the front door that Marnie seemed to become aware of her surroundings again and tried to pull away.

'No, McNeill, I can't go.'

'Sure you can. Come on. Look, Brutus is waiting.'

And as the dog chose then to catch hold of her sleeve in his mouth and pull her along, Marnie had to laugh.

'That's better,' McNeill said approvingly. 'You'd better take my arm, the road's a bit uneven.' Which was the only indication he gave that he'd noticed her clothes at all.

Morag's house was bright with lights and there was the sound of a piano being played. McNeill shepherded her inside, but Marnie flinched back as she saw that the room seemed half full of people who were busy talking and not listening to the pianist at all. A silence fell when she entered as everyone turned to look at her in open curiosity. She tried to turn to go out again, but McNeill was behind her and held her firmly by the arms. Then Katie called out a greeting and Morag came over to take her coat, and suddenly everyone was talking again and taking no notice of her.

'Welcome to the house,' Morag greeted her. 'Find yourselves some seats.' She took her coat and called over her shoulder, 'Hector, a dram for Ewan and Marnie.'

McNeill threaded his way to a vacant corner and Marnie sat down in an armchair while he perched on the arm, but Brutus disappeared into the kitchen where the drink was obviously kept. A pleasant-faced young man whom Marnie took to be Katie's fiancé brought them over a couple of drinks and then hurried to exchange greetings with some new arrivals. It was astonishing; Morag's house didn't seem to be much bigger than her own cottage and yet still more people were arriving.

Marnie looked at her drink suspiciously. 'What is it?'

'*Visge beatha*,' McNeill replied blandly.

'What on earth's that?'

'The water of life.'

Marnie raised her eyebrows. 'It doesn't look much like water.' She sniffed it experimentally. 'It's whisky.'

'Of course. What else would you expect the water of life to be?'

Marnie swirled the liquid in the glass for a moment, then took a good swallow. God, the stuff was neat! She choked a little, but the fiery spirit warmed her and her hands stopped shaking quite so much.

Behind her McNeill rested his arm along the back of the chair and putting his hand on her shoulder gave it a squeeze of encouragement. Marnie lifted her head to look at him and he grinned at her. She turned away quickly and sat forward so that he was no longer touching her, then took another long gulp of the raw spirit.

The evening became a kaleidoscope of sound and movement. Someone started to play a piano accordion and then an old, wizened man who reminded Marnie of a leprechaun joined in on the fiddle. Everybody began to sing but later fell quiet as a young girl took the centre of the floor and sang unaccompanied, her clear, sweet voice melody enough for the old Gaelic ballads, full of sadness and melancholy. But when she had laughingly refused to sing yet another song, the mood changed completely: chairs were pushed back, a space was cleared and people began to dance, not the reels and flings that Marnie expected, but just one, two or four people. A man was called on to do a sword dance, his 'swords' a pair of pokers from the fire, but he performed the intricate dance with inordinate skill, in and out of the swords, slowly at first but faster as the fiddler increased the tempo, until his feet seemed

hardly to be touching the floor. Everyone clapped and
shouted encouragement, but at length he had to stop,
exhausted, sinking on to a bench and taking great gulps
of the glass of beer that someone thrust into his hands.

Everyone was drinking freely, the women as well as
the men, and Marnie's glass never got to within a half
inch of the bottom before someone refilled it again. It
was very hot in the room; there must have been at
least thirty people there, and she would have loved a
glass of lemonade but didn't like to ask for it in case
Morag hadn't got any and she embarrassed her. An
old man told a funny story that involved a lot of strange
facial expressions and which had everyone in fits of
laughter, Marnie joining in even though she couldn't
understand a word of the Gaelic. There was more
dancing and Katie tried to make her join in, but she
wouldn't go, laughingly refusing and clinging to
McNeill's arm when Katie tried to pull her on to the
floor.

It was gone midnight before everyone grew too tired
to dance any more, and then they began to look towards
McNeill and call his name. He laughed and nodded
and the room grew quiet, everyone finding a seat and
making themselves comfortable. Brutus came into the
room, and pushed his way through the people who
were sitting on the floor and rested his head on
McNeill's knee. Somebody switched out the overhead
lights so that only a small lamp in the corner illumin-
ated the room, shining on the faces raised in anticipa-
tion. In soft, lilting Gaelic McNeill began to talk and
immediately his audience was spellbound, listening to
every word. What the story was Marnie couldn't tell,
but it was certainly dramatic and probably macabre,
she could see that from the expressions on their faces

and from the way that McNeill's voice changed tone becoming sinister and menacing as he built up the suspense and then sharp and staccato, words pouring out as fast as machine-gun bullets as he reached the climax. When he'd done there was a long, collective sigh, and everyone looked at their neighbour, grinning rather sheepishly and glad that they were going to have someone to walk home with through the dark night.

The *cèilidh* began to break up then; children were picked up off chairs where they had fallen asleep, coats put on, and goodnights exchanged. Marnie put down her for once empty glass and stood up to let McNeill help her on with her coat. Her legs were strangely unsteady after sitting for so long so that she swayed a little, and her voice felt slurry when she said goodnight to Morag and Katie. Outside the air felt cold after the fug of the heated room and she turned up the collar of her coat. McNeill folded her arm in his and held it firmly.

'Are you all right?'

'Mm, fine.' She looked up at the sky, her footsteps slowing. 'Look at all the stars, there must be millions of them. Far more than there are in London.'

'The air's clearer here, that's all. Come on.'

He pulled her gently, but Marnie stumbled on her high heels and had to cling to his arm. 'Am I drunk, McNeill?'

He laughed. 'No, but you've had enough to make you let down the barriers you've built around yourself.'

Marnie considered this as they walked slowly along. 'It's funny. I never tried drink. I haven't had a drink since . . .'

'Since when?'

She nearly said since the accident, nearly confided in him. But something held her back at the last moment and she said offhandedly, 'Oh—since ages ago.'

They walked on for a few minutes in silence, then Marnie stopped and turned to look at him. 'Did you deliberately set out to get me drunk tonight, McNeill?'

'Why don't you ever call me Ewan?' he countered.

Marnie frowned, considering it, then shrugged. 'I don't know. I always think of you as the McNeill man.'

'I see,' he observed, his voice heavy with self-irony.

'You haven't answered my question,' she prompted him.

'Did I set out to get you drunk? Why should I want to do that?'

'So that you could ... So that I wouldn't ... Oh, hell's bells, McNeill, why does any man ever want to get a girl drunk?'

'So that he can take advantage of her, presumably.' He looked at her derisively. 'Do you really think I have to stoop to that?'

Marnie lifted her head to study his lean, tough features outlined in the moonlight; the strong determined thrust of his jaw, the hard, almost cruel line of his mouth.

'No,' she said slowly. 'No, I don't.'

'Good.' His arm slid round her waist and he drew her to him. 'But drunk or not I intend to kiss you anyway.' And he did, expertly, and with his emotions held under a tight rein at first, as if he was afraid that she might indeed accuse him of taking advantage of her, but as Marnie returned his kiss, ardently, yearningly, he suddenly let go and took her mouth forcefully, bending her head back and kissing her with a fierce, raging hunger.

It was Marnie who drew away first, her breathing uneven as she clung to him. She leant her head against his shoulder and could feel his heart hammering in his chest. His arms were round her, holding her close against him.

After a few minutes, her voice unsteady, Marnie said, 'Do you—want me, McNeill?'

She felt his body jerk convulsively, then he answered harshly, 'Yes, I want you.' Taking hold of her arms, he pushed her a little away from him so that he could see her face. 'I've wanted to go to bed with you almost since the first time I saw you.'

Marnie could feel his fingers biting into her flesh, saw the flame of desire in his eyes. Lowering her head, she said haltingly, as if she found the words difficult, 'Then—what are you waiting for?' He started to say, 'Marnie . . .,' but she went on hurriedly, 'My place is nearest. Let's go there.'

McNeill was silent for a moment, but she couldn't look at him, was aware only of the moonlit darkness of the quiet night, of a slight breeze that gently ruffled her hair.

'All right.' He stooped and picked her up in his arms, carried her with long, impatient strides along the last few yards to her cottage and up the path, shouldered the door open and carried her with ease up the narrow staircase and into her bedroom. The fire she had lit there earlier had burnt low, but it still emitted a glow of orange light that flickered on the walls and the bed. McNeill set her down in front of it and kissed her again, then he began to undress her.

He did it slowly, taking his time, slipping her coat and then the jacket of her dress off and dropping them on a chair. His fingers caressed the bare skin of her arms, her shoulders, while his lips explored her throat and then brushed her mouth again, teasingly, tantalisingly. He found the straps of her dress and pulled them slowly off her shoulders and down her arms. Marnie shuddered and closed her eyes, knowing that he was looking at her, the fierce flame of hunger in his eyes. She turned suddenly with her back to him and put up her hands to cover her bare breasts. McNeill came up behind her and gently but firmly forced her hands away and replaced them with his own. Marnie gasped, then moaned as his fingers stroked, caressed. It was like the first time Alan had ever touched her there; she had been so young and so afraid at the reaction it had aroused in them both.

She jerked forward suddenly and stepped away from McNeill, pulling up her dress to cover herself and holding it in place with her hands. She stood between him and the fire, the light shining through her hair and giving her a golden, glowing aureole. Her voice high and hysterical, she said on a sob, 'I can't! I'm sorry, but I can't,' and turned away from him again.

McNeill stared at her, made as if he was going to grab hold of her and drag her back, but checked himself, his jaw tightening as he fought to regain his control. Fists tight clenched, he said at last, his voice harsh and ragged, 'Why not?'

'Because . . . because there's someone else.'

'I see. Who is he?'

Marnie hesitated, but the question had come out like a whiplash and wasn't to be denied. 'He is—was my fiancé.'

'Was?'

'He—broke it off. Found someone else.' Somehow

she said it although the words caught in her throat.

'How long were you engaged?'

'Six years. There was never anyone else.'

'Dear God!'

He came up behind her again, but this time gently
turned her round to face him. He kissed her on the
forehead as he would a friend or relation. 'It's all right,
Marnie, you don't have to be afraid. Go to bed and get
some sleep.' Then he turned abruptly and left her
alone.

The warm spell vanished overnight and the next few
days were wet and windy, the sky an ever-changing
mass of racing grey cloudscapes. On Sundays the
people of Culla only went outside to church, no one
worked except to tend to their animals and there were
no social visits, but on Monday Marnie was able to
catch the bus and go into Ardsay, stopping on the way
back at Morag's house to thank her for the *cèilidh*. Katie
immediately buttonholed her to ask her advice about a
wedding-dress and the two girls spent a pleasant hour
on their knees looking through pattern books that Katie
had borrowed from a dressmaker in Ardsay.

'She's got the material in,' Katie told Marnie, 'and
she can make up the dress in three or four days.'

'How long to the wedding?'

'It's a week on Saturday.'

'That's cutting it a bit fine, isn't it? You're lucky the
dressmaker can do it so quickly.'

'Oh, no, Mrs Murray's very quick. And I wanted to
wait until she got the new pattern books in.' Katie
turned to Marnie. 'You will come to the wedding,
won't you?'

'Of course.'

'You promise? And you'll help me to get ready?'

Marnie smiled at her. 'I promise.'

Morag had been taking advantage of the wet weather, when it had been impossible to work on her croft, in baking what seemed like a Ben Nevis of scones and oatcakes. She brought in a plate of them now, piping hot and dripping with butter.

'Did Ewan see you home all right on Saturday?' Morag asked with a casual air that didn't at all hide her curiosity.

Marnie flushed a little. 'Yes, thank you.' Adding, 'I'm afraid I was a little unsteady on my feet, though. I'm not used to drinking neat whisky.'

'Are you not?' Morag exclaimed in surprise. 'I thought they drank it all the time in London. They do on the television, anyway. Did Ewan tell you he was away to London himself?'

'Why, no.' Marnie looked at her in surprise. 'When's he going?'

'He's gone already. And on the Sabbath, too,' she added disapprovingly. 'He dropped a note through my door when we were away to church. It said he had to go and see his publishers and would be away for a few days.'

Their talk turned then to other things and soon Marnie took her leave. She looked at McNeill's house as she walked up the road, noticing that there was no smoke coming from the chimney but that the Land Rover was still there. He must have gone over in his own boat then and not waited for the mail-boat. It seemed strange not to have him there and she felt oddly lonely. She wondered why he hadn't told her he was going away, but supposed it had hardly been the time for idle chitchat after she'd made such a fool of herself on Saturday night. She flushed hotly as she remembered; she must have been completely mad—or drunk. Yes, put it down to the drink. But that still wouldn't be able to help her to look McNeill in the face the next time she saw him.

It was too wet and misty to go up into the hills, but on the Tuesday of the next week Marnie walked down to the beach wishing that she had Brutus to throw sticks for. The boat was still missing, but she was rewarded with her first view of seals, their grey heads popping in and out of the waves like corks. She walked along the edge of the water, feeling the salty rain on her face, the cold clean air on her cheeks. The sea was a heavy slate colour as the tide surged in, humping itself into a menacing swell against the cliffs. The bay was stark and hard, peopled only by herself and the seabirds, wheeling through the wind-torn skies. Slowly Marnie turned and walked back inland; the beach was too lonely and harsh a place to be alone today.

As she neared the house she saw the figure of a man, his back towards her, sheltering under the tiny porch, the collar of his overcoat turned up against the wind. For a moment she thought it was McNeill, but he was too tall, and besides, he never wore an overcoat. She hurried on, her footsteps lost in the wind, and pushed the gate open. Her visitor heard it creak and turned towards her. Marnie's hand stayed frozen on the gate. She stared, eyes wide in a face gone suddenly ashen.

'Hallo, Marnie.' Her ex-fiancé walked towards her and said, 'What on earth possessed you to come to a Godforsaken place like this?'

CHAPTER EIGHT

STILL holding on to the gate for support, Marnie stared at Alan unbelievingly. Her first feelings, once the numb shock of seeing him had receded a little, were of fear and resentment and hope all mixed up together. Fear that he had come to be cruel to her again, to accuse her once more of Sue's death, resentment that he had shattered the fragile peace of mind that she was beginning to build for herself, and somewhere, just a small spark at the back of her mind, hope that he had forgiven her and . . . But beyond that she was afraid to think.

He came towards her now, smiling, the way she always remembered, with an oddly lopsided grin. 'It's all right, it really is me. I'm not a ghost.' He stopped at the other side of the gate, his hands in his pockets, serious now as he looked at her searchingly. 'How are you, Marnie? You look—different, somehow.'

'Do I?' With a tremendous effort of will she managed to pull herself together. 'I'm fine. And you?'

He shrugged. 'As you see.' His hand came up to cover hers and he said softly, 'It's been a long time, Marnie.'

She looked down at his hand, said rather chokily, 'Yes.'

Alan looked up at the sky and smiled rather ruefully, 'Let's go inside, shall we? This is hardly the place to hold a conversation.'

'Yes, of course.' Marnie pushed open the gate and he stood aside to let her pass. He had a suitcase with him, a big navy holdall type, which he moved out of the way so that she could get to the door and push it open.

'Good lord, was it unlocked all the time? When there was no answer I just presumed that it was locked and didn't try the handle.' He dropped his bag on the floor and turned to shut the door.

'Were you waiting long?' Marnie's voice was uneven and nervous.

'About an hour. I got a taxi up from the harbour.'

'I'm sorry. Nobody locks their doors on Culla. You'd better take off your coat. I'll make some coffee.' She found that she wanted to look at him but was afraid to, and that her hands had begun to shake with nervous tension, so that she was glad of the excuse to go in the kitchen and do something. She took off her outer things and thought that she must look a mess, without make-up and her hair all over the place. Abstractedly she tried to straighten it while she made the coffee, but the kettle boiled all too quickly and she had to go and face him again.

He was standing, gazing into the fire, but he turned as she came in and stood watching her.

Marnie set down the tray and said stiltedly, 'I expect you'd prefer something stronger after that wait in the rain, but I'm afraid I haven't anything in the house.'

'It doesn't matter. Marnie,' he paused, waited until she looked at him. 'Come here.'

She straightened up, stood trembling, but didn't move.

Alan held out his arms to her, the way he'd so often done in the past. 'Darling!'

Marnie gave a great sob and rushed to him, put her

arms round his neck and clung to him while he held her close.

'Oh, sweetheart, why on earth didn't you let us know where you'd gone? We were looking for you for so long, were so worried.'

'I thought you didn't want me. I thought you all hated me for . . . for what I did,' Marnie sobbed out, tears coursing down her cheeks.

'No, never that. How could we possibly hate you?' He held her a little apart from him, smiled at her tenderly and bent to kiss her, long and lingeringly. 'There, does that convince you that I don't hate you?'

Marnie smiled at him tremulously. 'Yes, I—I suppose it does.' Then she frowned anxiously again. 'But Daddy? And my stepmother?'

Alan took her arm and led her to the settee, sat down beside her, his arm round her waist. 'Your father was shattered by what happened, but he didn't blame you, he blamed himself. He felt that he should have seen what was happening between—between Sue and me and put a stop to it, or at least given you some warning. Don't you see, darling, he felt that what happened was his fault and he could hardly bear to face you?'

Marnie looked at her hands, tightly folded in her lap. 'When I was in hospital he—neither of them—came to see me.'

'No, because your father was ill himself. He had a mild heart attack, but you weren't told because it was felt that it would only make you worse.'

'A heart attack?' Marnie stared at Alan in horror. 'Is he all right now?'

'Yes, he's fine. And only waiting for you to phone

up and talk to him before the two of them go off on a long cruise in the sun.'

'Really? You're sure?'

'Quite sure.'

Slowly Marnie relaxed a little, but then said tightly, 'And you? You didn't come to visit me in hospital either.'

'No.' Alan reached out and took hold of her hand. 'And I know that I was despicably cruel to you after Sue's funeral.' He hesitated, as if trying to find the right words, his eyes troubled. 'But you see I was in what I suppose you'd call a state of shock, with my whole world turned upside down. Even before the—the accident, I'd been getting pretty fed-up and frustrated because you wouldn't settle down and get married. Then Sue was—well, she was there and available. There was really no excuse for what happened. I felt rotten afterwards and told her it was over, but then she told me about the baby.' He paused and a bitter note came into his voice. 'Telling you was one of the hardest things I've ever had to do, but I have to admit that I'd made up my mind to it, that I'd accepted that my life was to be with Sue and the child. But then she died and everything blew up in my face again. And at the funeral—well, I'm afraid I took it out on you. Thought that if only you'd married me earlier none of it would have happened.'

Marnie stood up abruptly and moved away from him. 'Why don't you say it? You mean, or if I'd gone to bed with you.'

'Perhaps. But I never asked you to.'

'No. Why didn't you, Alan?'

He spread his hands and shrugged. 'Possibly because I have old-fashioned ideas about marriage. Possibly because I thought that if you were willing to go to bed with me then you might also be tempted to sleep with someone else.'

Marnie looked at him in surprise. 'I wouldn't have done that.'

'No, I know.' A fed-up look came into his eyes. 'I was a fool. Those petting sessions we had only made me more frustrated. I should have made you sleep with me.'

'Yes, maybe you should.' Marnie turned and stared out of the window, noticing that there was still no smoke coming from McNeill's chimney. He'd been away a long time. She turned back into the room and said with forced lightness, 'But you haven't had your coffee. Here, I'll pour it out for you. And I'll make up the fire. I expect you find it cold here after England?'

'It certainly is. It was quite summery when I left London.' He took the cup she offered him and asked, 'Why did you pick this place to run away to?'

Marnie shrugged. 'I just wanted somewhere quiet. I saw the advert for this cottage in a magazine.' She sat on the rug in front of the fire and leant back against the armchair, opposite Alan. 'How did you find me?'

He put down his cup and concentrated on stirring it again. 'Your father and I finally managed to make your solicitor part with your address. He'd always fobbed us off by saying that you were all right, but then your father came the heavy on him and threatened to go to court, so in the end he gave in and told us where you were. I arranged for my partner to cover the practice for a while and came over here as fast as I could.' He looked across at her. 'We've all been very worried about you, Marnie. Your friends, too.'

'Yes, of course.'

'You sound as if you don't believe it.'

'Of course I do. It's nice to know.' She stood up. 'Would you like another cup of coffee?'

'No.' Alan, too, stood up. He crossed to her and took hold of her hands. 'Marnie, I don't know how to say this, but I've missed you damnably. These last few months have been hell; knowing what a fool I'd been and worrying that I'd hurt you so much. It was quite a relief, I can tell you, finding you here safe and well, when I thought that . . . But that doesn't matter, you obviously are very well.' Marnie raised her eyes to look at him then quickly lowered them again.

'What I'm trying to say is,' he went on, 'that I'm sorry for blaming you for what happened. I'm over the shock of it all now and things have—well, fallen back into place again. And I want you to know that I never stopped loving you. Even when I—when I was with Sue, I was pretending it was you.'

'Stop it! How can you say that?' Marnie jerked her hands away.

'But it's true! Darling, please believe me. I want us to be engaged again, only this time there'll be no waiting, we'll get married straight away.' He caught her in his arms and kissed her fiercely. 'Oh, Marnie, you're so lovely. So beautiful. Say you'll forgive me. Oh, darling, I need you so desperately!'

Marnie kissed him back, tears of happiness in her eyes. 'Oh, Alan, I've been so lonely, so miserable!'

'But you'll never be unhappy again—I swear it.' He smiled down at her. 'We'll leave here tomorrow and get married just as soon as it can be arranged.'

Laughing, her eyes bright with excitement, Marnie said, 'Yes, we'll do that,' but then put a hand to her mouth. 'Oh, but I can't. I promised Katie I'd go to her wedding.'

Alan looked at her impatiently. 'Can't you cancel it? Surely your own wedding is more important?'

'But I must go, Alan. I promised I'd help her to get ready.'

'When is it?'

'On Saturday.'

'Well, I suppose that isn't too long to wait. In the meantime you'd better wear this.' He fished in his pocket and brought out a ring. 'Your engagement ring. I kept it when you sent it back. Even then I couldn't bring myself to get rid of it. Here, give me your hand.'

But Marnie was staring down at the ring, re-membering so many things. She lifted suddenly troubled eyes to his. 'No, you keep it for me until— until we go home again.'

'All right.' He put it back in his pocket and smiled at her, confidently, triumphantly. 'And maybe waiting here for a few days isn't such a bad idea after all. It will be wonderful to be alone together.' He kissed her and said softly, 'We'll be able to have two honey-moons—one before and one after the wedding.'

Marnie let him kiss her and then stepped back. 'I'm afraid it isn't as easy as all that. The Cullans are a very moral people. As soon as my neighbour gets to know you're here—which she probably has already, knowing the way gossip spreads round here—she'll send her daughter up to sleep here and act as chaperon.'

A look of dismay came over Alan's face and he groaned, 'You're not serious?'

'I'm afraid so. Perhaps it might be better if you arranged to stay at a hotel in Ardsay and just came out here during the day?'

He immediately began to argue, but in the end
Marnie had her way and he reluctantly agreed. So later
she walked down to Morag's house and asked if she
could use the phone, then arranged for Alan's hotel
accommodation and the taxi to take him there. That
Morag had unashamedly listened to her side of the
conversation, and was longing to know more, Marnie
was well aware, but she merely said that a friend had
called to see her. Later that evening, after dinner,
she saw Alan off in the taxi and stood at the gate
looking after him. Even then she didn't know why
she'd lied about Morag making Katie come to stay; she
knew that Morag would have disapproved of Alan
staying all night, but she would never have inter-
fered. No, it had been her own reluctance to commit
herself so quickly, not only to being back with Adam
on the old footing, but to go even further and become lovers. Somehow it seemed wrong, after all that
had happened, for him to just walk in and claim her
again.

The next day Alan hired a car and drove out early.
They went first to the Post Office in Ardsay where
Marnie had an emotional but very wonderful telephone
conversation with her father, and then on a tour of the
island, going over some of the roads that she remembered she'd covered with McNeill. She was about
to mention it, but then stopped, thinking that perhaps
Alan might not understand about McNeill. He kissed
her often that day, wanted to caress her and take
things further when they got back, but Marnie held
him off, told him, truthfully, that she needed a little
more time.

On Friday morning Marnie had another visitor;
Brutus pushed open the back door and bounded round

her excitedly, putting his front paws on her shoulders so that he was taller than she was and licking her face ecstatically, his tail wagging frantically and sending a packet of cornflakes cascading over the floor.

'Yes, I'm happy to see you again, too, but you're just too big for my kitchen.' She pushed him away and gave him some biscuits in a bowl, stood and watched him wolf them down in two seconds flat and gave him some more. So McNeill was back. She wondered what business it could have been to keep him away for so long. Had he finished his book and taken it over to his publishers himself? Discussed a new one while he was there, perhaps? But he'd got back in time for Katie's wedding. Yes, he wouldn't want to miss that.

Alan walked in as she stood there and Brutus looked up at him suspiciously, then returned to the last of the packet of biscuits.

'This is Brutus,' Marnie told him.

Alan gave the dog a cursory glance. 'A fine animal. So your neighbour's back, is he?' He turned and smiled at her. 'The weather's clearing at last. Let's take a picnic and our swimming things and find a quiet beach somewhere, shall we?' He chivvied her along, making her laugh at his impatience and they were ready to go in ten minutes, leaving Brutus looking forlornly after them as they drove away. That day Alan was even more importuning, trying to make love to her on the beach and again when they got back in the evening.

They had been lying on the hearthrug in front of the fire and at last Alan pushed himself away from her and sat up angrily. 'Why don't you come right out and say it?' he demanded bitterly. 'You just don't want to.'

Marnie too sat up and pulled down her sweater with shaking hands. 'I—I don't know. Please, Alan, I'm sorry. But I feel so—so mixed up. I've loved you for so long. I know I want to—but something keeps holding me back. I'm sorry,' she said again, miserably.

'It's probably not your fault.' He ran a hand through his hair. 'We both held back for so long before that it's become a habit, formed a psychological barrier or something. But God, I hope you can get over it when we're married.'

'I'm sure I will—but let's wait till then, shall we?' Marnie asked pleadingly.

'All right, if that's what you want.' He sounded tired. Getting to his feet, he added, 'I'd better be going. I'll call for you tomorrow as usual and we can go into Ardsay and book our tickets for the Monday ferry.'

'Yes, all right, but I'll have to be back in time to help Katie get ready. You're invited to the wedding, by the way; Morag called in last night after you'd gone.'

'I suppose the whole island's going?'

Marnie smiled. 'Most of them, I expect.'

The wedding wasn't until the afternoon, but as soon as Marnie got back from Ardsay the next morning she went round to Katie's house and washed and blow-dried her hair for her, then skilfully made up her face, using all the expertise she'd acquired over the years as a model. Nothing too elaborate, but bringing out all Katie's best features and highlighting the beauty of her soft brown eyes. When she'd finished Katie stared at herself in the mirror unbelievingly.

'Is that really me?'

Marnie laughingly assured her that it was. 'I'd better go home and get ready myself now. I'll come back and pin your cap on at about two o'clock, shall I?'

'Yes, that will be fine.' Katie was twisting round to

look at her side view in the mirror. 'It's lucky I am that you're a model, Marnie. I'd never have been able to do it myself. I would have looked just as I always do, but I so wanted to look special for Hector today.'

'You'll knock him off his feet. Now I must run or I won't be back in time.' Marnie turned and hurried down the stairs, then stopped suddenly, wondering how Katie had known she was a model. She hesitated, on the point of going back to ask, but then went on; she could always ask Katie later. She called goodbye to Morag, let herself out of the front door and almost bumped into McNeill, who was coming up the path.

'Oh! Hi.' Marnie's cheeks flushed as she remembered their last meeting and she said quickly, 'Did you have a good trip to England?'

'I achieved what I set out to do.' His grey eyes searched her face. 'You look very happy.'

Marnie smiled. 'Do I? I suppose that's because something—rather wonderful has happened since you've been away.' She moved to go past him. 'I must rush. I promised Katie I'd be back at two. See you at the wedding.'

McNeill stepped aside, but as she passed suddenly put out an arm and caught her shoulder, turning her round to face him. 'Marnie, are you really happy?' he said urgently, his voice sounding strained and tense.

She looked up at him in surprise. 'Why, yes, of course.'

For a moment he seemed as if he was about to say something, then merely nodded curtly and let her go, immediately turning and going on into the house.

Marnie gazed after him with a frown, then shrugged and went on her way.

She changed quickly and applied her own make-up

in half the time she'd taken to do Katie's, but she knew what to use on her own face, which base suited her skin and what shadows enhanced her eyes. The only thing she had suitable to wear was a turquoise blue suit with a darker coloured matching blouse. Marnie looked at it rather ruefully, wishing now that she hadn't sold or given away quite so many of her clothes, but it would have to do. Carefully she did her hair in the latest swept-back look and clipped it up at the back, adding, as an afterthought, a spray of forget-me-knots threaded among the clips, their tiny flowerheads exactly matching her suit and the blue of her eyes.

At two she was back at Morag's house and found Katie wearing her beautiful white dress, standing quite cool and serene among a bevy of female relations who were fussing round her. But she shooed them all out while Marnie pinned her flowered Juliet-cap headdress in place and arranged her veil over it.

Marnie stood back and smiled. 'There. Take a look.'

Slowly Katie turned to look at her reflection. After a long moment she said softly, 'Aye, I think I'll do.'

'That is the understatement of the year,' Marnie laughed. 'You look lovely, Katie. Really beautiful.'

'Thanks to you. I'm very grateful, Marnie. Oh, there's the cars arriving now.'

'I'd better go.' Marnie picked up her bag, then remembered and turned back at the door. 'Oh, by the way, Katie, how did you know I was a model?'

'Mm? Oh, Ewan told me.'

'McNeill? But how did he . . .' She saw that Katie wasn't listening and let it go. It didn't really matter anyway.

She drove to the church in Ardsay with some of Morag's relatives and found Alan waiting for her at

the door. They went in and sat at the back, most of the
guests having already arrived. Nearly all the men were
in Highland dress, the rich tartans of their kilts and
plaids making bright patches of colour in the sunlit
church. Katie was on time, and the look of pride on
Hector's face as he turned to greet his bride confirmed
to all the world that she was indeed very special.

After the ceremony the congregation stood while the
bridal couple walked down the aisle followed by the
principal guests. Marnie received a radiant smile from
Katie as she went by, but then Marnie caught her
breath. McNeill was just coming out of one of the front
pews and offering his arm to a middle-aged relative of
Morag's. He looked magnificent! Taller and broader
that most of the men, the dress tartan, with its black,
silver buttoned jacket, white shirt with frilled cravat
and cuffs, the bright red of the swirling kilt and the
plaid slung across his shoulders, all suited him perfectly. He was the quintessence of Highland manhood,
as tall and strong as his warrior ancestors. And his face,
too, was like granite. His eyes, cold as the winter tide,
settled for a moment on Marnie, then briefly on Alan,
then he looked away without any acknowledgement of
the smile she gave him. It was as if they weren't even
there, and Marnie felt suddenly cold and deflated.

The reception was at a local hotel where they dined
on fresh salmon caught in the local waters. There were
lots of telegrams, speeches and toasts, their wine
glasses being continually refilled throughout the meal,
then the tables were cleared away and the real business
of the day began as everyone settled down for a splen-
did *cèilidh*. This time there was far more space and
several men had brought their bagpipes, so, after Katie
and Hector had opened the dancing with a bridal reel

danced only by themselves, the best man and the chief bridesmaid, amidst a shower of confetti, everyone came on to the floor and they began to dance spirited Highland flings, reels and strathspeys. McNeill, too, joined in, dancing lightly and gracefully for all his size, his kilt swirling about his bare knees, the silver hilt of the *skean-dhu*, the small dirk stuck in the top of his sock, gleaming in the light as he moved.

As mere Sassenachs, Marnie and Alan sat and watched, but as the evening progressed and the dancing became more boisterous they were pulled to their feet and made to join in one of the reels. Marnie found herself, breathless and laughing, opposite McNeill. He swung her round on his arm, first one way, then the other. She leant back against his arm, felt it strong round her waist, and raised her head to look at him. There was a set look to his mouth, a strange kind of sadness in his eyes. Marnie saw it for only a moment and then it was gone, a mask coming over his face like a curtain pulled over a window.

Abruptly he pulled her out of the dance. 'Let's have a drink.' He led her to a quiet corner and got her a long, cool glass of lemonade. 'The flowers are starting to come out of your hair.'

He gently pushed them back into place and his fingers rested for a moment on her neck. His touch seemed to burn through her skin. His voice curt almost, he said, 'You look very lovely today.'

'Thank you.' Marnie looked at him in surprise. He'd never paid her a compliment before.

'I take it that the man you're with is the one you told me about?'

'Yes.' Marnie coloured, remembered what a fool she'd made of herself.

'And I presume he's come to take you back to England?'

'That's the general idea.'

'To get married?'

'Yes.'

'I see.' He turned to look at the dancers, 'It's the last reel. Watch—see where Katie's dancing. Soon some of the girls will come and steal her away and another will take her place to cheat the fairies in case they try to steal the bride for themselves. Then, after a while, Hector will look round and see that Katie has disappeared, and then his friends will lead him away and one of them take his place to fool the fairies again. He paused and put his hand on her shoulder. 'Then his friends will undress the groom and take him along to the bride's room where she'll already have been undressed by her friends and be waiting, then they'll leave them alone together.' He stopped and for a moment his hand tightened on her shoulder, bit fiercely into her flesh. Then he said curtly, 'Excuse me,' and walked away.

After the last reel, with its ancient, pagan ceremony, the party began to break up. Alan came to her side and said, 'You could do with a coat; there's a gale blowing outside.' Even during the hours while they'd been in the hotel celebrating the wedding, the unpredictable weather had changed and the wind was howling fiercely over the island. 'Better wait here while I get the car,' Alan advised. 'I won't be long.'

He went away and some laughing guests pushed past Marnie to go out of the door. Someone held the door open for an elderly man to pass through, but suddenly the wind snatched it and blew it out of his hand, smashing into the old man and sending him flying, down the flight of stone steps. There were cries of horror and the poor man was quickly picked up and brought back inside, his head bleeding and groaning in pain. Marnie took one look at the blood and turned quickly away, her nails biting into her palms, but she couldn't move away because of the press of people.

Word of the accident quickly spread and the doctor, who had been a guest, was soon bending over the injured man. McNeill pushed his way through to Marnie and took hold of her hand, putting his broad shoulders between her and the scene. Marnie clung to his hand tightly, remembering suddenly how he'd come and found her when she'd been hurt.

She heard the doctor say, 'He'll have to be taken to hospital straight away. Somebody phone up and ask to have an air ambulance flown over from Skye.'

Everyone began to murmur and comment while the hotel manager made the call and the injured man's relatives were comforted by the other guests. There was a blast of wind as the door opened again and then Alan appeared at her side. McNeill immediately let go of her hands.

'What happened?' Alan demanded. Swiftly Marnie told him, but he only seemed to be listening with half an ear, his eyes on McNeill.

'Well, there's nothing we can do. Come on, I've got the car outside. We might as well go.'

He went to pull Marnie away, but she drew back. 'No, we can't just walk by him, Alan. We must wait until he's moved.' Somehow Marnie knew that everyone would think them rude and unfeeling if they just left. It was part of the Highland character that everyone felt that they must stay and give comfort to the man's relations by their presence and sympathy.

The manager came back into the entrance and shook his head worriedly. 'The planes can't take off. The storm is even worse than this in Skye and there's no way they can get off the ground until it's died down.'

'Which way's the wind heading?' someone asked, and for a few minutes their talk was of wind force and tides, then someone said, 'A fast boat might make it, but it'll be risky.'

'Then we'll have to take the chance. He must be operated on without delay.'

There was a silence and Marnie found herself somehow compelled to look up into McNeill's face. For a moment their eyes met and held, then she felt him briefly touch her hand. He said, 'Take care of Brutus for me,' and turned his back on her. 'My boat's in the harbour here; I'll take him.'

Everything happened at once then; two men volunteered to go with him, someone found a blanket to wrap round the old man, and McNeill picked him up and gently carried him out of the hotel, most of the male guests following, leaving the women to bemoan such a sad ending to such a happy day. That, and for the womenfolk of the men who'd gone with McNeill to sit and wait for news of their safe arrival.

Alan took Marnie home shortly after and she collected Brutus from McNeill's house. After reminding her to do her packing the next day, ready to catch the mailboat on Monday, Alan left and she got ready for bed. But she couldn't sleep, just lay restlessly in bed, listening to the storm, howling and shrieking round the house. Brutus, too, seemed to sense that something was wrong and came to lie on the floor beside the bed, his ears constantly lifting at the slightest sound.

In the morning Marnie got up early and went to

Morag's house to find out if there was any news, battling her way against the storm and hanging on to Brutus' collar for support.

'No, there's none,' Morag told her anxiously, automatically pouring her out a cup of tea. 'But that's not to mean that they haven't got to Skye. The phone lines are down somewhere on Culla and when I sent young Willy Cameron down to the Post Office for news he said that they couldn't get through to anywhere, not Skye or Lewis or the mainland. It often happens when there's a bad storm, the cable carrying the lines under the sea get affected.'

Twice more during the day Marnie fought her way through the storm to Morag's house, but there was still no news. In the evening Alan drove out and found her sitting by the fire, gazing into it, the radio on but the reception so bad that it wasn't much more than continuous crackling.

'How can you listen to that?' he protested. 'Turn it off.' He looked round as she obeyed. 'Where are your cases? Are they upstairs?'

Marnie stood up nervously. 'The mail-boat probably won't be able to get here tomorrow, not in this storm.'

'No, curse it. I've had about enough of this place.' He came to her and kissed her. 'I want to get you away from here and back home where you belong.' He went to kiss her again, but she turned her head away. 'What is it?'

Marnie clenched her fists and took a deep breath. 'I'm sorry, Alan, but I'm not going with you.'

He stared at her. 'What do you mean?'

Desperately she sought for words, but there was no easy way to say it. 'I realised that I'm not in love with you any longer and I don't want to marry you. I . . .'

But Alan had caught hold of her shoulders and was glaring down at her. 'What the hell are you talking about?' he demanded fiercely. 'Of course you want to marry me. You *said* so.'

'No, I—I just wanted to be at peace with myself. I thought that by being engaged to you again I'd be happy, but I see now that all I really wanted was not to have you and my parents blaming me for what happened, to know that you didn't hate me. I tried to go back to before—before Sue was killed.' She stopped, floundering, lost for words. 'I'm sorry,' was all she could find to add.

Alan pulled her towards him, tried to hold her in his arms. 'We've been in love since you were seventeen. You can't just suddenly change over night. Yesterday you wanted to go home and get married, today you want to break it all off. What the hell happened in between?'

Gently Marnie drew away. 'Nothing. I think I just gradually fell out of love with you. It started happening a long time ago, but I didn't realise it; perhaps that was why I was in no hurry to get married.' She shook her head miserably. 'I don't know, Alan, all I know is that I'm not in love with you now.'

He turned and took a couple of violent paces round the room, then swung back to her. 'This is crazy. You're just doing it as some mad way of trying to punish me for making love to Sue. I've explained and apologised for that already. What the hell do you want me to do—go down on my knees and beg forgiveness?'

Marnie looked at him in horror. 'It has nothing to do with that.'

'No?' He glared at her. 'Well, maybe it is better if we end it all. I'd have to live the rest of my life knowing that you would always throw Sue's name back at me every time we had a row.'

Distress in her eyes, Marnie could only plead, 'Oh, don't be like this, Alan, please. You know I'd never do that.'

'No.' He sat down heavily on the settee, looking tired and drawn. 'I'm sorry, I'm not taking this very well, am I?' He put a hand up to his head. 'So I've lost both of you. I should have known. But I had to take the chance.'

Marnie looked at him in some bewilderment. 'I don't understand.'

'Don't you?' He stood up and came towards her. 'Marnie, please, for all that we meant to each other in the past, won't you reconsider?' She looked down unhappily, biting her lip, and he said, 'I shouldn't have asked that of you, it's obvious that you've made up your mind. So I'll say goodbye.'

He put out his hand to take hers, then suddenly pulled her into his arms and kissed her brutally, bending her back over his arm. Letting her go just as suddenly, he laughed harshly. 'What the hell am I trying to prove? I left it too late, I should have taken you long ago.' He turned and strode out of the room, and presently she heard his car start up and return back down the road to Ardsay.

It was three days before the storm abated enough for the mail-boat to make the island, but by that time there had been a radio message to say that McNeill and the other men had landed safely on Skye and that the injured man had been operated on successfully, although McNeill's boat had suffered some damage while they'd been trying to dock.

Marnie walked down to the pier with Brutus. Alan

was there waiting to catch the boat and Marnie looked at him uncertainly, but he came across immediately. He held her hand for a long moment, then ran up the gangplank as soon as it was in place, pushing aside the people who were trying to get off.

Quite a crowd had gathered on the pier and they surged forward to call a welcome as the men who had gone with McNeill disembarked. They greeted the women with kisses and pumped the men by the hand, glad to be back after their enforced stay on Skye. Marnie looked for McNeill, but when she didn't see him with the others went to ask one of the men where he was.

'Och, lassie, he's staying in Skye a while longer till he gets his boat repaired. He said to tell you to give the dog to Morag Ferguson to look after till he was home.'

'Oh. It's all right, I'll look after Brutus. Thank you.' She smiled at the man and he went off with his family.

The boat pulled out and she stood on the pier and watched it out of sight; she owed Alan that much.

The violent storm seemed to be the presage of summer, for after it came a spell of hot sunny weather and the first of the many tourists to invade the island. 'Bed and Breakfast' signs appeared from nowhere and blossomed on the most unlikely-looking crofts. Morag, ever practical, spring-cleaned Katie's old room and let it to a student botanist who had come to study and draw the wild flowers. One couple knocked on Marnie's door, but retreated rapidly at the sight of Brutus, but it made her decide to go over to McNeill's house and lock the door just in case some visitors should decide to take advantage of its empty state.

At first she couldn't find the key and had to search

around for it, eventually finding it in the kitchen drawer. While she was there she decided to check to make sure that everything was okay and went into all the rooms. In the main bedroom she saw some things he'd left lying around and tidied them away: a sweater, a notebook, a pair of gold cufflinks which presumably he'd found too heavy to wear with his black velvet jacket. Marnie wondered what he was wearing now, whether he'd brought some more casual clothes in Skye.

She opened the top drawer of his dresser to look for a box for the links and then stopped abruptly. Inside the drawer was a folder, one of the large envelope type in yellow manilla. Printed on it in large, neat letters were two words: 'MARNIE ADAMS'.

Slowly Marnie lifted the folder from the drawer, hands trembling, then carried it over to the bed and opened it. At the front of the folder were several photographs of herself torn from a recent copy of a glossy up-market monthly magazine. She was modelling winter furs and the photographs had been taken last November, almost her last job before the accident, although the magazine hadn't come out until January. In one shot she was wearing very high heels and a black mink coat, the skirt of the coat slightly parted to give the impression that she was wearing nothing underneath. She looked very sophisticated, very sexy, and very beautiful. On the margin of the first photograph someone had written two London phone numbers. One Marnie didn't recognise but guessed to be the number of the magazine, but the second was all too familiar; it was the number of the model agency that handled all her assignments.

On impulse she picked up the receiver of the bedside

extension and after some delay was connected with the agency. They were pleased to hear from her, wanted to know when she was coming back to work, and it was some time before she could put her own questions. Had anyone been enquiring about her lately? Had anyone asked personal questions?

Yes, they said, quite a few people had wanted her to model for them, and there had been several calls from people claiming to be her friends wanting to know where she was, but the agency had been unable to say and had refused to give any information about her background. Marnie thanked them and put down the phone, cutting short their repeated demands to know when she was coming back to work.

Marnie looked at the torn out pages thoughtfully: it looked as if McNeill had recognised her photograph and had then called the magazine to find out which agency she was with, but whatever he had tried to find out about her had been baulked by the agency's refusal to give personal details. So what had he done then? She took out the rest of the folder's contents and spread them on the bed. First was a letter dated shortly after McNeill had left for England and addressed to him in London. It was from a press cutting agency and stated that as they had only a short time at their disposal they had been able to come up with only the enclosed cuttings which they hoped would be satisfactory. Clipped to the letter were several photographs and items from society magazines showing her at some of the more fashionable parties and charity functions she'd attended, including one where Alan had been her escort; an item from a newspaper gossip column linking her name with a man she'd only ever dated once and hadn't seen since, and, last of all, newspaper clippings from the more sensational papers giving a luridly detailed account of the accident with photographs of herself, Sue and Alan.

Feeling slightly stunned and sick, Marnie sat and stared at them. So McNeill knew, had deliberately tried to find out all he could about her while he was in London. And had succeeded very well by the look of it; there wasn't much the papers hadn't found out, they'd even hinted at the rift with Alan, although fortunately no one seemed to know about Sue and the baby. But why had McNeill gone to all the trouble to find out about her? To what purpose? Marnie frowned as she puzzled over the problem. There were still two pieces of paper she hadn't looked at. She picked them up and suddenly things began to become very clear. The first sheet of notepaper had two addresses jotted down on it in McNeill's handwriting: those of her parents and Alan. The second was a street map of her home town. He had marked a route on it from the nearest motorway—but not to her parents' house—his neat arrows led to Alan's surgery.

As the implications began to sink in, Marnie turned to the phone again and dialled her solicitor. No, they told her, they had followed her instructions implicitly and had not divulged her address to her father or anyone. They seemed rather put out that she should think they might have done.

Marnie put down the receiver and a lot of little things she hadn't taken much notice of at the time began to fall into place: the fact that Alan had known who Brutus belonged to before she'd said, and Brutus recognising Alan, not treating him as a stranger. McNeill must have taken the dog with him when he went to see Alan. About what? To tell him where she was, obviously. And Alan had come at once, had arrived in Culla before McNeill got back, and the two men had then ignored one another, treated each other as strangers so that she wouldn't find out. But why? Why had McNeill gone to all that trouble to get her ex-fiancé to come to her? Because she'd told McNeill that she still loved Alan, presumably.

Marnie stood up and began to pace the floor as she tried to work it out. Did McNeill see himself as some sort of fairy godfather, getting them together and patching up her broken romance? But somehow that didn't sound like McNeill at all; he was the type to stand back and let people sort out their own problems rather than interfere where he wasn't involved. So did that mean that he considered himself to *be* involved? Marnie stopped pacing and stared at the bed. He'd said he wanted her, had wanted her from the first moment he'd met her, but she'd rejected him because of Alan. And almost immediately McNeill had left Culla, found out where Alan was and sent him back to her. *Why?* Because he was sorry for her and wanted her to be happy? Or because—Marnie sat down suddenly on the bed—or because he wanted her to find out for herself whether she was *really* still in love with Alan or only with the memory of what they'd once felt?

She sat for a long time on the bed, gazing abstractedly into space, then she slowly, carefully, put all the papers back in the folder and replaced it in the drawer before letting herself out of the house.

Marnie sat on the clifftop with Brutus stretched out beside her. A slight breeze ruffled the rich green grass, and made the heads of the daisies dance like miniature ballerinas. Overhead the seabirds flew, the bright sunlight shining through their translucent wings against a brilliant blue sky, the colours all so vivid, so intense that they hurt the eyes. She had been up here for several hours now watching the cool, early light slanting across the rippled sand of the beach; watching the tide change from being just a diamond-bright line far out to a full, powerful force that gradually ate away the sand and crept up the shore. They had shared some sandwiches and a couple of apples between them, she and the dog, and for a while Marnie had leant her head on his long back and used him as a pillow while she dozed a little in the sun. But the nearing thud of the waves had woken her and she had sat up to watch and wait as she'd waited yesterday and the day before.

The tide reached its peak and began to turn again, and almost she gave up and went home, but then, far out to sea on the horizon, she saw a white speck that gradually enlarged into a boat coming fast into the bay. Immediately Marnie stood up and began to head back downhill, the dog loping along beside her.

She reached the bay just as McNeill was tying the dinghy to the jetty and slowed her steps, recovering her breath while the dog rushed forward in exuberant greeting, barking and his tail wagging nineteen to the dozen in his joy at seeing his master again. McNeill stood it for a few minutes, then lifted the dog's paws from his shoulders and held him by the collar. He looked at Marnie for a long moment and then said, 'Hallo, Marnie. I didn't expect to see you here.' He walked slowly towards her, the dog at his heels still trembling with excitement.

Her voice husky, Marnie looked up at him and smiled. 'Hallo, McNeill. Welcome home.'

He stiffened and a shadow crossed his eyes. Turning, he began to walk up the beach and Marnie fell into step beside him. For a while they walked in silence, then McNeill said abruptly, 'What happened to the boy-friend?'

Her face averted, Marnie answered as calmly as she could, 'He went home.'

She felt him give her a quick glance. 'Why didn't you go with him?'

Slowly Marnie turned her head to look at him, at his hard features that seemed a little thinner than before, at the tough, set line of his jaw. 'Because you asked me to look after Brutus for you.'

He came to a stop and jerked round to face her. 'You stayed on because of that?'

'Partly. And partly because I changed my mind.'

His eyes narrowed. 'About what?'

'About leaving.' She turned and began to walk on again.

'Are you going to stay on here, then?'

'Yes, for the summer.' They reached the gate to McNeill's house and came to a stop.

'And you're going to wait till then to get married?' McNeill asked, an oddly harsh note in his voice.

'I'm not getting married after all.' Marnie pushed open the gate and walked ahead of him up the path. She opened the door and stepped inside, then turned and smiled at him again. '*Ceud mile fàilte*, McNeill.'

He stared at her for a moment, his eyes widening. 'Marnie . . .'

But she moved away from him into the sitting-room.

He pushed the front door shut and strode quickly after her. Marnie stood in the middle of the room and waited for him. The room seemed to shrink as he stepped inside. He took a swift glance round, noting that it was clean and bright, the vases full of wild flowers, the savoury aroma of a pie coming from the kitchen. He looked at her frowningly, for once uncertain.

Before he could speak Marnie said quickly, 'I want to apologise to you. When I first arrived on Culla I behaved very badly towards everyone. But you see, I'd been involved in an accident in which my sister was killed.'

He hesitated for a moment, then said gently, 'Yes, I know. I found out while I was in England.'

Steadily Marnie went on, 'Maybe some day I'll tell you all about that, but right now I just wanted to apologise for taking my bloody-mindedness out on you.'

McNeill shrugged. 'I just happened to be within firing range. But my shoulders are pretty broad, I can take it.'

Marnie let her eyes travel over the wide expanse of his chest and said rather thickly, 'Yes.'

He returned her gaze for a long moment, a great light slowly growing in his eyes. 'Does that mean what I think it does? What I want it to mean?'

'That rather depends on what you want, doesn't it?' Marnie managed in little more than a ragged whisper.

Reaching out, he gently drew her to him. 'This is what I want.' His eyes never leaving hers, he slowly lowered his head and found her mouth with his.

If he had any doubts left they were soon dispelled as Marnie returned his kiss with all the pent-up yearning of the long days of waiting, days in which she'd known that she loved him and had hoped agonisingly that his bringing Alan to Culla had meant that McNeill loved her. After the first startled moment of awareness, he caught her up tightly in his arms and kissed her with a savage hunger, all restraint abandoned, losing himself in her ardent sexuality.

'Oh, Marnie, *mo ghraidh*!' He kissed her eyes, her throat, then returned passionately to her bruised mouth. 'If you only knew what hell I've been going through since I had to leave here! I imagined you married to him already, making love . . .'

'Hush.' Marnie stretched up on tiptoe to stop his mouth with hers. 'It was your going away that made me fully understand my own feelings. When Alan arrived I felt terribly happy and I thought it was because I still loved him, but then I realised it was because I knew that he and my father didn't blame me for Sue's death. It was like a great weight being lifted off my shoulders. And it was only then, when I stopped feeling guilty, that I realised that I hadn't really been in love with Alan for quite some time.'

'And now?' he asked softly, already sure of her answer, but wanting to hear her say it.

Marnie smiled and put up a hand to gently trace the outline of his chin. She should have known that someone with a jaw like that wouldn't be content to just sit back and wait for her to come out of her unhappiness, to recover from her neurosis; he would chance his whole future on the throw of the dice, take the risk that he might lose her when she saw Alan again, but know that in doing so he had given back peace of mind and happiness to the girl he loved.

Steadily she answered, 'And now I know that I love you. That what I felt for Alan was only a youthful infatuation in comparison with this. And I know that

I'll go on loving you till the day I die.'

McNeill stared at her for a long moment, a great light of triumph and yet incredulity in his eyes, as if he couldn't yet believe that she was truly his. He kissed her very gently, almost humbly, then smiled at her teasingly. 'Don't you want to know whether I love you?'

Marnie stepped back, trying to conceal a smile. 'Oh, but I already knew.'

His eyebrows flew up. 'You did? How?'

'I remembered you called me *mo ghraidh* a couple of times and I asked Morag what it meant.' She flushed a little. 'Somehow I didn't think that you'd call a girl "my love" unless you really meant it, McNeill.'

He looked amused. 'You're right, I wouldn't.' He drew her towards him again and held her close, his hands low on her hips. 'But my name's Ewan, remember?'

'But I prefer McNeill. It's masculine and dominant, like an old clan laird.'

'Hmm. Come to think of it, I prefer Adams. It calls to mind the garden of Eden and fig leaves and . . .' He broke off and laughed as Marnie hit him playfully on the jaw, then became serious again. 'Darling. *A ghraidh mo chridhe*, love of my heart, I fell in love with you the first time I saw you smile; you looked like a flower that was afraid to bloom. I wanted to make you love me, but the only way I could ever make you come out of your apathy at all was by making you angry. I had to take the risk of making you hate me because it was the only emotion I *could* rouse in you. You were like a firework about to explode! But at least you began to learn to live again.'

'And then I made such a fool of myself after the

cèilidh.' Marnie reached up and put her arms round his neck. 'Maybe you should have insisted on making love to me that night.'

'No, I wasn't going to force you into something you weren't ready for. It had to be this way. Especially as I'd held back all the time you were staying here.'

'Why did you?'

He bent to kiss the tip of her nose. 'Because you were ill and because you were a guest in my house, of course.'

Marnie smiled. 'I'm neither of those things now.'

'So you're not. And if you don't stop moving against me like that I make no guarantees about waiting until we're married,' he told her unevenly.

'Will we be married here in Culla?'

'Yes. Marnie, will you stop . . .'

'And will we dance the bridal dance, and will our friends spirit us away to cheat the fairies? And will they undress us and then bring you to my bed?'

'Yes, all that, Marnie, for God's sake . . .'

'And will . . .'

But this time it was her words that were broken off as McNeill, unable to stand it any longer, roughly kissed her. Then he firmly picked her up in his arms and carried her upstairs.

Masquerade
Historical Romances

Intrigue
excitement
romance

BUCCANEER'S LADY
by Robyn Stuart

Corinna Barrett sailed to the West Indies to find her
missing father, but she was kidnapped and sold as a slave
to Captain Brandon Hawke before her search had really
begun. Yet why had Brandon insisted on buying her,
when he so clearly despised everything she stood for?

SUMMER HEIRESS
by Ann Hulme

Miss Aurelia Sinclair had just a year to save her
Jamaican sugar estates from her father's creditors, and
she was resolved to make a rich marriage. Unluckily,
she fell in love with Harry, Viscount Belphege — who
believed she was the heiress she had pretended to be!

Look out for these titles in your local paperback shop from
14th August 1981

The Mills & Boon Rose is the Rose of Romance

Every month there are ten new titles to choose from — ten new
stories about people falling in love, people you want to read
about, people in exciting, far-away places. Choose Mills & Boon.
It's your way of relaxing:

August's titles are:

COLLISION by *Margaret Pargeter*
After the heartless way Max Heger had treated her, Selena wanted
to be revenged on him. But things didn't work out as she had
planned.

DARK REMEMBRANCE by *Daphne Clair*
Could Raina marry Logan Thorne a year after her husband Perry's
death, when she knew that Perry would always come first with her?

AN APPLE FROM EVE by *Betty Neels*
Doctor Tane van Diederijk and his fiancée were always cropping
up in Euphemia's life. If only she could see the back of both of
them?

COPPER LAKE by *Kay Thorpe*
Everything was conspiring to get Toni engaged to Sean. But she
was in love with his brother Rafe — who had the worst possible
opinion of her!

INVISIBLE WIFE by *Jane Arbor*
Vicente Massimo blamed Tania for his brother's death. So how
was it that Tania soon found herself blackmailed into marrying him?

BACHELOR'S WIFE by *Jessica Steele*
Penny's marriage to Nash Devereux had been a ' paper ' one. So
why did Nash want a reconciliation just when Penny wanted to
marry Trevor?

CASTLE IN SPAIN by *Margaret Rome*
Did Birdie love the lordly Vulcan, Conde de la Conquista de Retz
— who wanted to marry her — or did she fear him?

KING OF CULLA by *Sally Wentworth*
After the death of her sister, Marnie wanted to be left alone.
But the forceful Ewan McNeill didn't seem to get the message!

ALWAYS THE BOSS by *Victoria Gordon*
The formidable Conan Garth was wrong in every opinion he held
of Dinah — but could she ever make him see it?

CONFIRMED BACHELOR by *Roberta Leigh*
Bradley Dexter was everything Robyn disliked. But now that she
could give him a well-deserved lesson, fate was playing tricks on
her!

If you have difficulty in obtaining any of these books from your
local paperback retailer, write to:

Mills & Boon Reader Service
P.O. Box 236, Thornton Road, Croydon, Surrey, CR9 3RU.
Available August 1981

Mills & Boon
Best Seller Romances

The very best of Mills & Boon Romances

brought back for those of you who missed

them when they were first published.

In August
we bring back the following four
great romantic titles.

STORMY HAVEN
by Rosalind Brett

When Melanie came to the island of Mindoa in the Indian
Ocean she was little more than a schoolgirl; when she left,
only eight months later, she had grown into a woman. Her
scheming cousin Elfrida, Ramon Perez and the masterful
Stephen Brent had all played their parts in this transforma-
tion.

BOSS MAN FROM OGALLALA
by Janet Dailey

Casey knew she was perfectly capable of running her father's
ranch for him while he was in hospital. It was *only* because
she was a girl that Flint McCallister had been brought in to do
the job. So what with one thing and another, there was hardly
a warm welcome waiting for the new boss!

DARK CASTLE
by Anne Mather

What Julie had once felt for Jonas Hunter was now past
history and she had made every effort to keep it so. But now
she found herself travelling to Scotland to make contact with
him again. Could she manage to remain on purely business
terms with the man who had meant so much to her and whose
attraction for her had increased rather than lessened?

THE GIRL AT DANES' DYKE
by Margaret Rome

'Women aren't welcome at Danes' Dyke,' the inscrutable
Thor Halden told Raine; nevertheless circumstances forced
him to take her under his roof for a time, and to persuade her
to masquerade as his wife. It was a difficult enough situation
for Raine, even before she found herself falling in love with
him. Would she ever be able to make him trust her?

If you have difficulty in obtaining any of these books through
your local paperback retailer, write to:
Mills & Boon Reader Service
P.O. Box 236, Thornton Road, Croydon, Surrey, CR9 3RU.

Three great Doctor Nurse Romances to look out for this month

There are now three Doctor Nurse Romances for you to look out for and enjoy every month.
These are the titles for August

CHATEAU NURSE
by Jan Haye

After an attack of pneumonia, Nurse Hilary Hope jumps at the chance of doing some private nursing in France but does not expect her life to be turned upside down by the local devastating doctor there, Raoul de la Rue . . .

HOSPITAL IN THE MOUNTAINS
by Jean Evans

After a terrible car accident, Nurse Jill Sinclair accompanies her injured brother to an Austrian clinic where Baron von Reimer hopes to repair his injuries. But the Doctor Baron is such an attractive man that Jill soon finds herself in an impossible situation . . .

OVER THE GREEN MASK
by Lisa Cooper

An exciting new part of her life begins when Nurse Jennifer Turner first reports at the Princess Beatrice Hospital — but nothing works out as she'd dreamed after she meets handsome registrar, Nicholas Smythe.